A TIME TO BURN

A TIME TO BURN

Timothy Ireland

First published in June 1992 by GMP Publishers Ltd
P O Box 247, London N17 9QR, England

World Copyright © 1992 Timothy Ireland

A CIP catalogue record for this book
is available from the British Library

ISBN 0 85449 176 7

Distributed in North America by InBook.
P O Box 120470, East Haven, CT 06512, USA

Distributed in Australia by Bulldog Books
P O Box 155, Broadway, NSW 2007, Australia

Printed and bound in the EC on environmentally-friendly paper
by Nørhaven A/S, Viborg, Denmark

DEDICATION TO

The Brighton Years and
John, The Compact Disc Man,
Hazel and Steve, for their friendship,
and the dark-eyed Geoff Bloomfield

I would also like to thank Ed for Paris, Jenny for Shame, Fiona for her
Shopping Lists, Chris Poole for our chats, Julie Scholes for getting me back,
Paul and Beccy for those inebriated Sunday Lunchtimes and Tony S. for
dancing with me. Thanks also to Brian Ralph despite the shortness of our
time together, Chris and John for The Aquarium and The Queen's Head,
and everyone at Secrets.

Finally, I would like to remember three who have died:

Richard Dipple, my editor, for his soft spoken and wise advice,
Brian Kennedy, whose 1983 rainbowed braces I have not forgotten, and
Soledad Tercero, dearest friend of the family.

His breath is smokey in the cold air.

For no reason it seems, he is remembering again. The memory casts a deeper chill. He looks out across the grey still water, shivering slightly.

Does anything, he wonders, ever really end...?

SLEDGEHAMMER

It should have been an ordinary day. Nothing seems amiss as John walks up the rain-washed path, glancing up at their first floor window where he'd expected to see a light. Instead there is only the ghost whiteness of the veiled curtains and darkness behind.

Black too are the windows of the deserted second floor flat. Debbie and Annette had moved out a month ago. Jeff still complained about missing them. He'd liked their chatter, the way they could talk about nothing for hours, legs entwined, plaiting each other's long hair, face to face like two cosy cats.

Inside the house on the first floor landing John feels for the keys, half expecting to hear music coming through the door. Jeff listened to the cassette-radio when he cooked, improvising dance-steps while he drained the pasta, slicing the peppers and tomatoes, his head bobbing in time to the latest beat. But this evening there is silence. Jeff must still be out.

Turning the large mortice-lock, John finds the Yale latch-key which surprisingly sticks fast in the lock. Refuses to budge.

'One good kick would break the lock,' Steve suggests, fifteen exasperating minutes later.

John considers his neighbour, a young man of twenty-eight who towers above him. Knowing Steve is a builder, he'd hoped for a practical but less aggressive solution. Resigned, John steps back from the door.

'Be my guest,' he says.

Steve scratches his two day old dark stubble.

'You sure?'

'Certain.'

Steve obliges with a hefty booted kick. John winces as the wood splinters and paintwork cracks. Gratifyingly, the security lock does not give way at once. Bracing the muscles developed by his work and regular weight training, Steve takes a breath and then delivers another elephant kick. The wood shudders, the lock gives way and the door swings open. His own male pride salvaged, Steve smiles sheepishly.

'Coffee...' John offers, the sense of relief making him doubly grateful.

He watches Steve wipe his forehead with the back of his hand. At least breaking into the flat has raised a little sweat.

'Thanks.'

The two men step into the hallway which is just as John had left it that morning. Leading the way into the living-room, John freezes in disbelief as he opens the stripped wood door to reveal chaos.

'Jesus Christ.' This is Steve, peering over his shoulder.

John can't say anything.

Everything has been turned upside down, as though a mean

wind has whirled in, snatching open the drawers of the dresser, the doors of the sideboard, hurling the contents onto the carpeted floor which is littered with letters and glasses, papers and photographs, table linen and souvenirs.

Sinking down onto his knees, John stares numbly at a framed photograph, distorted now by fractured glass. Why should anyone have broken this...? Cold, he picks the shards of glass out of the frame. His hands are shaking. Unsteadily, he stands up, unaware of the blood trickling down his fingers, and restores the black and white portrait to its proper place on top of the bookcase.

Steve returns from his search of the rest of the flat and, gentle in the moment, touches him lightly on the shoulders. Both are nervous of what they might see or reveal in their eyes.

'You'd better come and look,' Steve says slowly.

Like a child, John follows him through the narrow hall, passing the kitchen and spare bedroom which are completely untouched, to the main bedroom he shares.

They'd used a sledgehammer to get in. Battered their way through the hardboard, plaster and rafters. Narrow shards of wood hang down from the ceiling, adhered to by tatters of wallpaper and the black muzz of insulating fibre. In the centre of the ceiling is the jagged black hole through which they'd come.

Below, clothes are flung everywhere. Drawers from the mahogany chest have been pulled out and tipped over. Ties, vests, shirts, belts, underpants, handkerchieves, diaries, theatre programmes, love letters, photographs, KY jelly, cellotape, vitamins, soft pornography, foot powder, pyjamas, a cock-shaped dildo, ancient school reports, certificates, holiday brochures, jumpers, towels and socks: all have been turned out and rifled through. Dust from the broken plaster, chips of wood and flaps of paper add to the desolation. Worst of all, perhaps just before they left, they'd thrown back the duvet and urinated over the wide double bed. The pale blue sheets are still dark and wet.

'They must have broken into the upstairs flat first,' Steve muses. 'Maybe they knew Debbie and Annette had moved out.'

'Maybe...'

Numb, such details are irrelevant. John feels Steve looking at him, waiting for some reaction, some response that will amplify his outrage.

If only Jeff was here... John glances at his wristwatch, not really registering the time.

'Shall I call the police?' Steve's voice is husky with concern.

'I said I'd make coffee,' John begins.

'There's no need.'

Awkward, Steve shuffles his feet. As a witness, he feels he has a duty to stay. He cannot yet retreat downstairs to his own home and the motoring magazine he'd been reading when John had called.

'I should be getting you a drink.' Steve hesitates, wondering if it is whisky for shock.

John smiles the distracted smile of a madman.

'There's brandy in the living room. I'll get it.'

Busying himself, he picks his way through the wreckage, managing to find a bottle and glasses. Already he wonders if the flat will ever feel like home again. Standing in the kitchen, John passes Steve a tumbler with an inch of brandy and ice cubes from the freezer box. Although he seldom touches spirits, preferring lager, Steve takes a swallow out of politeness.

'Have they taken much?' he asks, curious now the worst of the discovery is over for him.

John shrugs. Somehow this isn't important.

'I noticed the TV was still there.'

'Yes...'

'Perhaps it was too heavy for them. With the high ceiling it would have been quite a struggle.'

Lost for a moment in his own conjecture, Steve considers the desk they'd carried from the spare bedroom with the hard chair balanced on top so that they were just able to climb out the way they'd forced themselves in.

The policeman, when he arrives at last, takes one look at the devastated ceiling and smiles.

'Never seen one like that before,' he says. 'Heard about it, sir, but never seen the evidence myself.'

John yawns. The awful events of the evening, coming at the end of a long day in the classroom, have exhausted him. All he wants now is to crawl into some warm corner and sleep. Only there is no safe place here any more.

The policeman, bright-eyed and smooth-skinned, with that polished face which men in that line of duty present to the public, looms over John in his thick dark navy uniform. It is a relief when he is gone.

Then Steve reappears, toolbag in hand.

'I've put the biggest padlock I could find on the upstair's flat's front door,' he says. 'So no intruders can pay a return visit.'

Surprised by such kindness, John can't think for a moment what to say. Like so many neighbours who live so close together they have had little enough to do with each other in the past.

'I'll fix the lock on your front door now,' Steve insists. 'Let you get on with the clearing up.'

John nods, only half listening.

Sorry for him, Steve pauses by the door.

'Your mate home soon?'

John makes himself shrug.

'I expect he's held up somewhere. In a pub with friends.'

It's hard to know where to start. First of all John strips the double bed, putting the sheets, pillowcases and duvet cover into the washing machine. With soapy disinfectant he sponges the damp stains on the mattress, appalled even while he cleans.

After Steve has fitted the new lock, John asks him to stay for a drink. Three large brandies later, Steve is slightly tipsy as he makes his farewell. John, who will be forty soon, feels almost fatherly as he shows the young man out, advising him to be careful on the stairs.

Checking his wristwatch, he sees it is just after eleven and still Jeff is not back. Although recently Jeff has once or twice stayed out until the early hours, always before he has left a message, made some excuse.

Turning his wavering attention to the upheaval in the living room, John starts putting the drawers back, haphazardly replacing the books and papers, stacking the letters and odds and ends into piles, sweeping up the broken glass. As he tidies and clears mechanically, forcing himself to work, he is half aware that things are missing. The drawers and cupboards aren't so full as they had been. There are even some books missing from the bookshelves. None of it makes much sense.

Kneeling in their bedroom, he begins to sort through the clothes that have been pulled out of drawers and the wardrobes. Nearly every garment is crumpled or dusty and the pile of things which need washing steadily increases as he sorts, his attention blurred by the trauma and the brandy.

Then underneath a coil of ties — red, blue, striped and paisley — he finds the letter. The letter which Jeff had originally left for him on the bedside table.

That had fluttered to the floor as the intruders had come and wrecked havoc. Nervous of his own name written in the familiar hand, he breaks the seal of the envelope, pulls out the few pages. Afterwards, he can only ever remember seeing three words. Words that jump out at him from the fourth or fifth line.

I'm so sorry

He looks away, knowing suddenly. The half empty cupboards. The gaps on the bookshelves. The crumpled pile of clothes that he sees now are only his own...

Jeff has left him.

AFTERWARDS

The time-set chatter of Capital Radio wakes John as usual. Not bothering to open his eyes, he rolls over, warm under the wide duvet. Still not fully awake, he reaches out just as he has on most of the last thousand mornings, but finds only a cold space. Opening his eyes, he sees the pillow beside him is smooth and undented. He is alone in their bed.

Usually he was the first to wake. He'd leave Jeff sleeping, rise and step naked to the bathroom. Slipping under the shower, he'd let the hot water play over his body and lazily soap himself, aware of the flicker of desire.

Turning over now onto his stomach, John closes his eyes and his body recalls the feel of Jeff beneath him; the fragile bones in his shoulders, the lean back...

Only yesterday Jeff had been here with him. He had showered while Jeff prepared a simple breakfast. Nothing had seemed amiss. There had been no arguments. No atmosphere he remembered. He'd left Jeff skimming *The Guardian* at the kitchen table.

Throwing back the duvet, John climbs out of bed, his nakedness goosepimpling despite the timed-set central heating. Going into the kitchen, he makes a solitary cup of tea. The glasses he's used for the brandy last night are still unwashed on the chrome draining board.

Jeff couldn't have foreseen the break-in. But had he planned his own escape for weeks...?

Uncomfortably, Johns looks about him. The imitation mahogany kitchen cupboards Jeff had chosen, and which made the kitchen dark, are all neatly shut. John opens them one by one, unable to stop himself.

Jeff has left the silver and white teapot behind, but the matching coffee pot is gone. As are three of the six silver and white cups and saucers. And half the long-stemmed wine glasses. Everything evenly split down the middle. Just like Jeff. The tidy one.

He can't remember the last time he had been late for work. Fortunately Sarah covers for him at Registration, but now the whole of IW are his. There are twenty-eight of them aged between eight and nine years. A racial mix of fifteen girls and thirteen boys. Generally the girls are the more troublesome.

He stares at them for a moment, struggling to focus on reality. Then the teacher he's been for nearly sixteen years takes over. He can almost feel one of his private selves turn over like a page inside him, and the all too familiar practised face appears.

'Sir...' Nadia, a flame-haired girl on Table Two, lifts one hand, ever ready to distract him.

Smiling for a moment, John rises from his desk and steps to the white wipe-off board with a thick blue erasable pen. This morning is the second session on Trees and the Environment.

As he returns from work, already the winter evening is beginning to draw in. He pauses outside the red-brick three-storey Victorian house, unable to stop himself from looking for a light at their window.

Things between us weren't the same any more. We both knew that.

So Jeff's letter read. But what did it mean? What had changed exactly? Perhaps lately they'd talked to each other less. Certainly, they'd made love less frequently and with less passion than before. But surely that happened to every couple after six years...

Lying on the wide double bed, John opens his eyes and sees the battered hole in the ceiling above him. The violence which caused this still appals him. Now, in the half-light, shadows seem to creep in through the jagged hole and the memories stir.

He tries to remember what had been real.

When the telephone rings he snatches up the receiver, the hope making him stumble.

But it is Suzi, his 'baby' sister.

'Everything all right then?' she asks, after a minute.

John hesitates. Something in his manner must have given him away.

'Is there anything wrong?'

He takes a breath.

'The flat's been broken into.'

Now Suzi pauses.

'*When?*' she says. 'When did this happen?'

She sounds as though she doesn't believe him, even though it was years since they'd been hooked on kidding each other with tantalizingly believable Tall Stories.

'Yesterday.'

'Did they take anything?'

'A portable cassette-radio. The silver cutlery Gran left me. My leather jacket. Some cash we kept in a drawer.'

The word *we* catches at him. There is a silence. Awkward, they wait for each other to speak.

'How is Jeff taking it?'

John swallows, torn between the truth and a lie.

'Jeff has left me.'

The quiet which follows these words makes John wonder if Suzi has heard him properly.

'What a bastard...' Suzi begins, then checks herself. 'When was this? Are you all right?'

Not answering, John suddenly remembers another time, years ago now, when his diminutive sister had physically shaken him. He sees again Suzi's pale, slightly triangular face, her brown bobbed hair electric with indignation. 'I want you to kill him,' she'd shouted, 'because it's the only way you'll get over it.'

He pushes the memory away.

'I'd come round,' he hears Suzi say, 'but it's Keith's club night at squash, so I'm minding the children.'

'How are they?'

'Asleep hopefully.' Suzi sighs. Just changing the subject has somehow altered things. Aware of this, she's irritated with herself for even mentioning her husband. John knows what she is thinking, but is actually relieved.

'You're welcome to come round here,' Suzi offers, knowing it is in vain.

'I'd rather be on my own right now.'

He says this as gently as he can. There is another pause. John can almost see Suzi glancing at her watch, thinking of the daughter who might need tucking into bed, the son who might at his hour still be playing in the darkness with the latest computer game.

'We'll meet over the weekend,' Suzi says. 'Promise.'

She hangs up, afraid she has said too little, still adjusting to the news.

It is the word *promise* which stays in John's head.

We were not happy, he thinks. Things had not been *happy* for the last two years, maybe longer. Maybe from the time they'd argued about the flat; who owned it, whose home it was. And the age gap — the same nine years which had seemed so insignificant when they'd first met — had lately begun to count. Perhaps Jeff, who always prized youth, had become afraid of a future with someone middle-aged.

Was there another lover? The letter did not say.

John moves close to the window that overlooks the back garden of Steve's ground floor flat. Although it is still February already the crocuses are showing, flurries of gold and white luminous now in the wintry darkness. Beyond the neighbouring garden stand the tall houses of the adjacent street. Chinks of electric light slip through folds in curtains or between slats in blinds. At one high-up window he sees a sexless, possibly naked figure cross a lighted room. From another there is the flickering glow of a television.

Then, gradually, he becomes aware of something else. He runs his hand against the cold glass.

It's as though someone is down there in the garden below. Pricking the corner of his consciousness is the disturbing sense of a figure standing in the shadows. Someone is watching him.

VISITING

Guy says he is better today. Chris says the same. John nods his head and tries not to notice how painfully thin Guy's arms are. The three of them are in a side room off a busy medical ward which has a name — Solomon Ward — rather than a number (D2, C1, E3), but which is no more homely. Chris has done his best, bringing in a cassette-radio, a portable TV, framed photographs, a large pink teddy bear and even a picture from home: a huge monochrome Marilyn Monroe.

Today Guy, recovering from the latest chest infection, sits up in bed supported by pillows and plays the ageing Hollywood starlet.

'Ahm jest playne bushed, honey,' he says in an attempt at a Southern belle. As he says this his fine hands push up imaginary tresses of hair.

When John first met Guy two years ago, Guy did in fact have long red hair skilfully permed and shoulder-length. Now his hair is pricked in short and gelled ginger spikes, but still he tosses his head and uses his hands to push back from his face the curls that are no longer there. These ghost-like movements fascinate John. He wonders if they are what he will remember most when Guy has gone.

'Who is this, Craig?' Guy says, drooping his lips in what is supposed to be a silky pout. In his hands he is holding the latest of the cards Chris has brought in.

'Duncan's friend,' answers Chris, who is always patient.

'Oh...the Po Face.' Guy grimaces and tosses the card down on the washed-out green NHS coverlet.

Retrieving it, Chris reaches over to the top of Guy's cluttered locker for a small ball of Blu-tack. He rolls the blue gum betwen his fingers before sticking this latest card to the wall opposite Guy's bed. There are now thirteen cards secured in this way. Less than there were the first time Guy was confined to hospital.

'Do you like my nightie, love?' Guy asks John. 'They'd run out of pyjamas. You know, NHS shortages, food parcels next. No, nursey, I say, Gina doesn't mind a gown. Gowns, I told her, were all Gina wore in her better days.'

Gina is what Guy calls himself. When he was part of a drag troupe touring the London pub circuit, Gina was his stage name. He has clung to it ever since, even though it is perhaps three years since he performed in a wig and a dress.

'I've brought in some pyjamas,' Chris says.

These are pink and designed for women. Wearing them Guy will look especially frail, his boney wrists brutal out of a frilled sleeve. The sporadic bouts of diarrhoea mean Guy has to change his bed attire several times a day. Each time he visits, Chris brings in freshly-laundered pyjamas, taking the soiled ones home in an elegantly-lettered Harrods bag.

Chris would like to look after Guy all day, but he has a serious and steady job in a towerblock office in the City. On several occasions already, John has had to persuade Chris not to resign from work. As he states the same arguments over again, once more temporarily convincing Chris, he goes away hoping he has done the right thing.

'It wasn't the cough that carried her off, it was the coffin they carried her off in.'

Guy smiles as he says this, watching Chris's face cloud almost with satisfaction. It is slightly bewildering to John, their relationship — the deliberate way Guy upsets Chris, who seldom complains, as if he is grateful for these bruises. John notes how Guy always watches Chris's face when he hurts him, intent on his expression. Perhaps this is a sign of love.

Coughing theatrically, Guy overdoes the performance and struggles for a moment to breathe. Chris moves closer to the bed, leaning forward out of the chair; a bald, bullish man of fifty, reaching for his young lover's hand. Guy, who is not yet twenty-five, draws his own hand away. He looks up and over at John with his watery blue eyes that he tells everyone are cornflower.

'Pardon Gina's chest infection,' Guy says. 'Dr Wotsit says Gina's better. Her crisis time has passed, he said. Lovely, I told him, Gina adores a crisis. Here today, pneumonia tomorrow.'

'He is better,' Chris says again. 'The doctor said he'd be back home in a couple of days.'

John nods uncomfortably. It isn't so much a fear of what is happening in this small room — although yes, he is afraid — but rather the sense that he is intruding on something too intimate to be observed. He feels this even though Guy and Chris seldom touch each other in any way when he is present.

Noticing Chris fidgeting with the Harrods bag that contains fresh pyjamas, John smiles at Guy who rolls his eyes as though it is a private joke, his lover's devotion.

23

'I'll leave you both in a minute,' John says.

'Right.' Chris frowns a little.

Guy waits until John is just by the door.

'You found yourself another man?' Guy says. 'I expect Janice has been through a dozen already.'

Janice is Guy's name for Jeff. Colouring a little, John shakes his head, struggling for a rueful grin.

'No man yet,' he says quietly, and leaves the room, pulling the door shut behind him.

That March night is the chilliest for several years. Frost leaves its feathered finger prints on the window. Even the swollen moon looks cold.

John wakes abruptly as though he has been disturbed. Shivering, he draws the duvet up over his shoulders. He has not slept well since the break-in. Is still not used to Jeff's absence. He keeps dreaming that the intruder returns. Every waking ending more violent than the last.

Before he would simply have rolled over, closed his eyes again, reached for the recumbent body beside him. Now he is restless, his senses curiously alert, straining for a sound.

Think of a holiday, he tells himself. Think of school tomorrow. Think of sex. Anything to shut out the nightmare.

Turning over, his heart beats faster. He tenses suddenly, his body rigid as a bone. He is sure he can hear footsteps on the stairs.

FORTY

The day ends like any other. Opening the front door quietly, John steps into the dim hallway. Putting his brief-case down, he hangs his coat up and then kneels down to pick up from his scratchy doormat the pile of post. Scanning the square white and blue and cream envelopes, he checks the handwriting, running through a short but reliable list of names. But the card he'd hoped for isn't there.

Telling himself he is foolish to be disappointed, he slips off his shoes. Padding into the kitchen in his socks, he hesitates before he switches on the kettle. Perhaps today of all days he should have treated himself to a bottle of wine.

As he opens the living room door, he blinks, startled because the room is flickering with candle light. Huge shadows are cast upon the walls and there are faces everywhere. Familiar faces made strange by the flames of the tall white candles each person is holding. There are perhaps twenty gathered here, nodding at him or smiling, their eyes like soft jewels made of tears make him shy. Nervous of them, he can almost hear the collective intake of breath as they all dip their heads, self-conscious as a group now, and begin to sing 'Happy Birthday' which starts shakily, just like any party, but ends with energy, relief and more laughter. Some venture a second chorus, but this quickly fades away and John is left there still speechless.

'Make a wish,' someone calls. It is Guy, gaunt in a tight black dress with a looping crimson scarf.

At once everyone in the room blows out their candles and for a moment the room is in complete darkness. This is perfect, John thinks, wondering what will happen next and forgetting until later to cast his wish. Then Suzi, who has stood watching proceedings from a corner of the room, switches on the light. Someone else puts an early Beatles record on the Hi-Fi and other people open bottles of wine and refill glasses. Everyone, except John, who has Eva throw her arms around him, starts talking at once.

Squeezed into a dark green sports jacket with an olive shirt and black leather tie, Chris — broad-shouldered, bullet-headed — is uncomfortable in the role of host. He'd been more than happy to help Suzi arrange this surprise party, but now circling his way through the clusters of mainly middle-aged people, he prefers refilling glasses to making conversation.

Glancing across the room he thinks how good John still looks. Although the black hair is thinning and streaked with grey now, a short haircut would help disguise that. And whilst the usual seductive moustache is presently missing, John's brown eyes are still catching.

Chris sighs.

Their friendship has been a gradual one, grown slowly over the fifteen years their paths have crossed in the North

London clubs and pubs, at parties and lamented tea dances, whilst shopping in the changing high street or loitering out of doors on summer evenings in the casual cruising grounds under the trees on Hampstead Heath or Primose Hill.

The two men exchange smiles across the crowded room. Chris recalls again John's startled face as he'd stumbled across his surprise party guests. The sheer bewilderment, as though he'd interrupted a seance, everyone holding hands in the darkness ready to call back the dead.

'I can't believe it,' Suzi says to her brother. 'Your fortieth birthday.'

Wrapped in a purple narrow-waisted dress with long filigree earrings and flat black shoes, she thinks how nice it is to dress up for a change.

'You love this,' John says, good-humouredly. 'For once you're thinking how pleased you are to be the baby sister. Another seven years before the Grim Reaper catches up with you.'

Suzi laughs, forgetting temporarily the children who are tonight in their father's sole care. In fact Keith is home at this very moment attempting to settle a restless Jodie with a bedtime story, waiting for Sean to be returned from his Karate class.

'Forty,' she says again. 'It's a good time to make a new start.'

She turns the fizzing long-stemmed glass around in her fingers as though it is a crystal ball.

'I've thought of moving.' John hesitates. This is the first time he's mentioned it to anyone.

Suzi adjusts her necklace.

'Letting go can only be a good thing,' she says, sounding as always so certain.

'Too many memories, you think.'

Suzi grimaces.

'At least you're free to change things,' she says.

He half smiles, unable to see why she should envy him the independence which lately feels more like loneliness. Taking one of the still-full bottles off the sideboard, he pours himself some more white wine, anticipating the blurring effects of the alcohol and then remembers Suzi's glass.

Replenished, Suzi makes a toast. They chink glasses dangerously. Does he ever realize just how much I love him, Suzi wonders.

Later, as he listens to Sarah, a friend and fellow teacher, he becomes aware over the cynical melodies of Joe Jackson that someone is calling out his name. Unsteadily, he turns towards the voice. It's Ed, a teacher from his previous school. He smiles, trying to think of something to say, and then sees that Ed is holding up the receiver of the telephone.

'Hello,' he says twice.

But the voice that he can just hear over the music and the chatter is completely unfamiliar.

Everyone who sees the laughter die out of John's face is sure the telephone call is from Jeff.

Bright smiles of forced interest from loyal friends, and muted whispers of speculation from those unable to help themselves, dissipates in different ways the awkwardness of John's sudden exit from the room. Fuelled by alcohol, gossip and professional common ground, the party carries on. When the front doorbell of the flat rings twenty minutes later, heralding a new unexpected arrival, one or two of the guests even hold their breath. But it's not Jeff who has come.

It is Guy who starts the rumour that the newcomer — a young man in denim jacket and jeans who circles uncertainly with his glass of wine appearing not to know anyone there — is, in fact, a Stripper.

'They sent a denim cowboy,' Guy improvises, toying with his long crimson scarf. 'I was hoping for a Leatherman, heavenly chunky thighs and a high voice.' He corners the fascinated Eva by the bookshelves. 'He won't go all the way...' Guy reassures her. 'Cock is extra. Just down to the G-string and the cowboy hat. Apparently his stage name's Lucky Star.'

Suzi, who has not yet heard this mischief, watches the young man, aware of his awkwardness and wonders, jealously, if this is John's new lover. This new arrival is attractive, the blue denim suits him, but he badly needs a shave.

In the sanctuary of the narrow kitchen, quite unaware of the ripples caused by his neighbour Steve's entrance, John leans back against the pinboard on the wall and closes his eyes. The voice at the end of the telephone had been an older woman's, loud with uncertainty.

'It's Rachel Headington,' she'd said.

Even the name meant nothing to him.

'We met once,' the woman had continued. 'Many years ago. Probably you won't remember. I'm Ralph's sister.'

'Ralph...?'

For just a moment he is stupid. Perhaps because it was all so long ago.

Ralph.

Then, more than anything he wants to be alone, but the collection of friends and acquaintances will be here in his flat for a while yet. He can hardly tell them all to go away.

The kitchen door flies open, making him start. Eva, worried suddenly that John might not appreciate the joke, bursts in to warn him.

'Do you realize a stripper's here?' she asks.

Even now he does not need the glass of wine which stands beside his solitary dinner plate. Effortlessly, he goes back...

RALPH

Two men with moon faces lean against each other, weighted in space by heavy brown suits and solemn eyes. Next to the Picasso is a Van Gogh. The eternal yellow chair bright against a turquoise background. Over the chipped and flaking door hangs the poster he'd made with Rosalyn. Green and red and yellow handprints, Rosalyn's smaller than his, arranged like flowers, their fingers petals, and underneath written in bold letters, the word PEACE.

He takes in the details of the cramped bed-sitting room slowly, not wanting to return yet.

Like other young men he'd wished for an older lover; dreamed of Zeus rather than Adonis.

Miraculously, Ralph had come, stalking him silently through the colourful, aromatic market stalls in Portobello Road one Saturday afternoon, until at last they had exchanged nervous smiles.

Broad-shouldered, his god has the suspicion of grey in his beard — the grey that sneaks in between the thirtieth and fortieth year — and a thick, circumcised cock he will only later discover is of above average proportions.

Dwarfed by Ralph, he is narrow-hipped and trim-waisted as a boy. Caught in the arms of his grizzled warrior, a virgin at nineteen, he is the innocent Ralph wants him to be. With tenderness and care, taking his time, Ralph is the first to violate every orifice. When this benediction is done, both of them rest until it can begin again.

The two men with moon faces see it all and say nothing. The pleasure goes on. Ralph's cock, but more exquisitely, his fingers and tongue, are shy of nothing. Rocked in the strong arms of this being so utterly male, he writhes under the goose touch of Ralph's belly, crying out even as the rhythm deepens, his lips burned by Ralph's beard.

Thin-ribbed as an Indian, he sits cross-legged on the dusty brown carpet of his bed-sitting room. Pushing back the black hair which hangs down over this boney shoulders in two thick swathes, he smokes a cigarette very slowly, flicking ash into an empty milk bottle in a practised way. Behind him, prostrate on the twisted sheets of the narrow bed his lover lies lost in the deep sleep of the sated.

Often he imagines Ralph is not one man, but many; the sum of all the different Ralphs there have been in thirty-seven years. He sings, giddy at the weight of their embraces. It's as though in loving Ralph he possesses time. He sits there humming, light-headed, drunk on all those days and months and years that are his now.

Abruptly, the light fades. The curtains flail in the gathering breeze. Suddenly sombre, the sky casts a shadow even into his room. He stands up, naked like a sacrifice. Outside the black clouds rise like smoke. Drawn to the window, he waits in the falling darkness for the flash of electricity over the distant roofs. Closer, making him shiver, comes the shattering rumble of thunder as the heavens break.

Leaning out of the upstairs window, he feels the fierce spatter of wet drops on his face and bare shoulders. Breathing in the smell of the rain and the perfume of the flowers, he looks down at the night-scented stocks ghostly-white like coral, encrusted in the dark on the window-boxes of the flat below.

Then Ralph, disturbed by the storm, is behind him, drawing him back from the window and the rain into the soft blackness of the room and an embrace, flesh against bone, which turns into a mocking and tender slow dance.

He can feel Ralph against him, the beard pressed to his cheek, now to his throat, caressing. Their arms are round each other, his linked round Ralph's neck. As they turn those soft steps, a lazy pretend waltz, Ralph's hands wander down his lean back. So sure the fingers feel, how strong the hands. And Ralph's kiss...

At first he doesn't recognize the emaciated man who is lying in bed six, dressed in the sickly orange pyjamas that hospitals loan to patients.

He is hollow-cheeked, his chin pushed heavily forward onto his chest by an excess of pillows supposed to make him comfortable. There is a brown stain, gravy or old blood, on one of the sleeves which hang loosely around his thin arms. Not only clean-shaven, the man seems shorter than Ralph was and narrow-shouldered. Surely the nurse he had spoken to has made some mistake...

He gets up to call someone and his hard chair squeaks against the tiled floor. The man in the bed opens his eyes. His eyes are still blue.

'Ralph...'

The man in the bed turns his head slowly towards the new voice. Even this slight movement appears to cause him pain.

'*John*...?' The man's voice is perceptibly slurred.

'Yes.'

The blue eyes gradually pull him into focus. Sitting back down on the hard chair, John is aware of the visitors clustered around the adjacent beds; husbands and wives, daughters and grandsons. Reaching out, he takes hold of Ralph's wasted hand and notices a thin, transparent tube coiling out from under the creased sheet to a syringe trapped in a small metal pump. A green light flickers every second, metering out the prescribed dose.

'Are you comfortable?'

Ralph nods, then closes his eyes for a moment.

'Just some bad dreams.' He tries to smile. 'I thought it made you high.'

'Perhaps they can change the drug.'

'No point.'

To soften these words which are said simply, Ralph attempts to squeeze John's hand. The Ralph of before had had a handshake which could crush your fingers.

'You know it's cancer...'

John nods.

'I was afraid it was the Big A. Losing so much weight. Kept away from the Doc. They say it's too late to operate. Too widespread for chemotherapy.'

John takes a breath.

'Best thing really,' Ralph manages. 'I wouldn't want to be cut about. They say I'm on a waiting list. For a hospice.'

'Rachel told me.'

Shakily, Ralph raises a hand, tries to sit forward a little.

'What happened to your lovely long hair?' he asks.

'When it started to turn grey, it also began to fall out.'

Ralph touches his own chin with his fingers.

'You see the beard's gone...' he says.

John nods.

Is that the trick of time, he wonders, to humble you?

The giant redwood trees make them both seem small, vulnerably human. The sky arches above them in a tumbling line of blue. It's an autumn afternoon. The light September breeze casts a chill. He shivers as he steps under the shadow of another redwood. They'd gone out without coats that afternoon, perhaps for the last time that year. He'd wanted Ralph to hold him.

'This has stood here a hundred years,' Ralph says, running his wide hands down the ribbed rust bark, his fingers searching the dark uneven grooves made by nature. They wander on a little further to a secluded spot which becomes their own enclave. Sinking to his knees, Ralph runs his hands palm down over the soft turf.

Later, he kneels down on the grass.

'We could have a garden,' he says, with more emphasis.

John wonders why the word *we* frightens him. He takes a breath. So newly free, light-footed with the sense of life out there waiting for him, the commitment Ralph requires is like a curtain that shuts the wide perspective off, confining him to four walls.

The September afternoon in Kew Gardens is lost to him.

Again he is in William's house. He can hear their voices coming now from the front room, seeping down the hallway like water, trickling into his ears. Ralph and the host and the host's friend.

In the kitchen where he shelters, high up and running round all four walls, is a narrow wooden shelf upon which there sits a bowl of apples, each perfectly green, perfectly round and all made of china. Next to this, inside a glass case, secure amongst stiff weed, is the silver disc of a stuffed fish, red-finned and glassy-eyed. And then a bowl of oranges, perfectly coloured, perfectly shaped and made of wax. And another dead thing fixed behind the glass.

He'd knotted Ralph's tie that evening, he standing, while Ralph sat on a hard chair. He'd often do things like that, small services, perhaps ironing a shirt, kneeling over to remove Ralph's shoes, unconsciously playing out a pantomime of boy and master — or was it simply lover and loved... He remembers lifting Ralph's shirt collar, looping the blue paisley tie around his neck, when Ralph's hands, taking his wrists firmly and gently at the same time, had stopped him. He remembers Ralph looking up at him, his blue-eyed god with a black beard stumbling over the right words.

'I know you wanted time...' Ralph begins.

'We both did.'

He lets the tie go, steps away, out of reach of Ralph's arms. Checking his wrist watch, he avoids Ralph's eyes.

'We're late already,' he says.

Julian accepts their apologies, ushering them into the front room where they both shy away from the reflections which loom down at them from the tall, gilt-framed mirror over the tiled fireplace. Uttering pleasantries, they try to make themselves comfortable on the hard classic green and silver striped settees. In his late twenties, Julian teaches Latin and History at a private girls' school in St John's Wood. William, more than twenty years his senior, had once nearly been someone grand on the London theatre scene and now has the distinguished featured face which looks good in black and white and secures him small parts on television. William takes Ralph's arm, reclaiming him for the evening.

'My dear boy, you never get a day older,' William says.

John turns away, imagining Ralph and William as the lovers they had once been more than a decade ago. In such imaginings William is always as old as he is now: grey-haired, pot-bellied and thin-legged. The picture disgusts him. If only Ralph could stay thirty-seven forever.

He starts as Julian touches his arm lightly, blinks at him through the oval gold-framed spectacles. So fair his hair is almost white, Julian is permanently pink-skinned. John thinks of William touching Julian's boyish pink skin, stroking it with those awful vein-knotted hands. He tries to smile as Julian clears his throat and gestures to the record-player in the corner of the room. Muted in the background for the sake of conversation moans a symphony by Mahler. John does not know which symphony it is, but Ralph has told him several times how William had discovered Mahler for him. Now Julian smiles, the beardless chin so smooth you might almost suspect that Julian never needed to shave.

'We can have the Beatles or the Beach Boys,' Julian says. 'William is trying to convert me to pop.'

And so the evening unravels until he is standing on his own in the kitchen surrounded by bowls of perfectly shaped, perfectly coloured apples, bananas, oranges, lemons and pears. And between each display frozen forever behind the panes of glass something dead — a fish, an owl, a fox cub — looks at him with lifeless eyes.

He waits for Ralph to come. It's as though an invisible stopwatch is ticking away the seconds and the minutes, clicking inside Ralph's head even while he makes polite conversation, sips his wine and acknowledges the pop music that William has fashionably decided to play. At a certain point, when the seconds and minutes have built up into a question, Ralph will wonder where John is. He will come and look for him.

John sighs, a curiously strangled sound.

If only he could go back, rejoin the little social circle, smile quickly at Ralph over the brim of his glass, wait for William to include him temporarily in the conversation, laugh even at the right places, picking up the cues which William feeds everyone like an old hand. If only he could return to his place on the settee beside Julian and sit tight and wait for the evening to pass, then Ralph would not need to find him and the words which are running now, casting shadows over everything they do or say, will not be said. And Ralph will be his for a little while longer.

He takes a breath, wishing he was anywhere else. For here in William's house he cannot be gentle. He resents the way William controls the evening, turning them all into puppets. He hates the fact that William and Ralph share a past that has nothing to do with him. He wishes he could simply forbid Ralph from ever seeing William again, but is afraid that such a demand would jeopardize even Ralph's love — the same love that seeks to surround and possess him as though it were absolute.

'Why?' Ralph asks. 'Why are you doing this?'

There is more hurt than anger in his voice. John can

hardly breathe.

'I was bored.'

He makes his own voice insolent. Although it is the last thing in the world he wants to do, he sees he will have to hurt Ralph if he is to get free.

'William isn't important,' Ralph argues. 'It's us, you and me, that counts.'

These words intimidate him. How tempting it is to move over closer to his lover. It only needs a few steps and then Ralph will hold him, perhaps forever. But forever can seem like oblivion.

'I'm only twenty-one...' John says.

There is a silence. He can remember, even after all these years, how that silence seemed to go on for hours. Ralph frowns, as though he hasn't heard, bewildered as a bear, at one moment lord of the wood, whose leg has been caught in the jaws of a trap.

They stand as though fixed in time.

'I want you to live with me,' Ralph says.

There is the clatter of footsteps across the shiny floor as a nurse hurries by on some errand. They tighten their grip on each other's hands.

'Another four years and I would have retired.' Ralph frowns. 'Perhaps that would have been more daunting than this.'

He pulls up the blue NHS coverlet, disturbing the syringe-pump with the flickering green light.

'You could have taken up gardening,' John says. 'Runner beans and tomatoes. Bought a dog.'

Ralph smiles at this as John intended.

'I'm not so much afraid,' he begins. 'It's just the thought of everything coming to an end. Never being in my own place again.'

'Couldn't Rachel or I arrange to take you home?'

Ralph shakes his head.

'I've said goodbye to the house. Said goodbye to most of the people I wanted to. You took some tracking down.'

Easing himself onto his back, his face is grey with effort.

'It was Rachel who persevered,' he says. 'Even though she doesn't quite approve.'

He closes his eyes for a long moment, then stirs.

'We had some good times.' A ghost of a smile hovers on the cracked lips. 'You still remember?'

'Yes...'

It feels a lifetime ago. It is too late now to speak of love, of the chances they had once had as lovers. John swallows, choked by a surge of regret. The unalterable fact was that he had turned Ralph away. So young then, he'd seen only the possibilities of freedom rather than the limits. Had not known how quickly the years could slip through your fingers, how very few were the lovers who might lastingly love. As perhaps Ralph would have.

But the cruellest thing of all is that he knows he could have passed this dying man on the street and not even recognized him. You were like a god to me... he thinks. He looks down. Ralph's face twists as though the pain is closer still.

'Shall I get a nurse?'

Ralph nods and at the same time, reaches out for him.

'Say goodbye now,' he whispers.

The party—carefully planned the day before Christmas Eve so that even those going away for the holiday couldn't cry off — is in full swing. Standing in the hallway that is hung with holly and lit with candles, he can hear William's voice booming as though he is still on stage, the practised laugh ringing on and on, demanding attention.

As he takes off his coat, Julian, blinking at him through his gold-framed spectacles, assures him that there will be carols later, that everyone must join in. John smiles politely. He can imagine Julian seated at the grand piano in the drawing room with William behind him leading the chorus, the cultivated bass voice drowning out Julian's tenor.

He suspects now that William had invited him out of spite, made Julian his messenger.

Trying to disguise his nerves, he waits in the hall for Julian to lead him into the long living room. As he stands in the doorway under the festive mistletoe, he takes a breath and forces himself to look round at the milling guests.

But Ralph is not there.

He shuts the white door and locks it. Like a murderer he takes off Julian's oval gold-rimmed spectacles so his victim cannot see him. He wonders what he is doing here, hiding in the second upstairs bathroom with someone he feels nothing for. Giddy with alcohol, bruised by the sense of loss, he fumbles with the buttons of Julian's blue shirt, pulls down the grey herringbone trousers with their neat creases, runs his hands over Julian's smooth, milky body.

It is a sort of violence which makes him hard. He has never penetrated a man before. Guided by Julian, he enters him roughly, surprised how good it feels, the pleasure in the brutish thrusting, the satisfaction of Julian's small cries like imitations of pain. He thinks how powerless he has been before, dominated by Ralph, yet enjoying Ralph's possession of him. Only he had lost Ralph to someone else now... Digging his nails into Julian's back, he bites Julian's neck, deliberately leaving marks for William to find.

Unable to go back to sleep, he stands naked at the kitchen window. The dawn light suddenly seems harsh, exposing a pattern of veins in his thigh. He shivers. This memory of William and Julian has been locked away for half his lifetime, yet he can still feel dirtied by it.

Reboiling the kettle, he reaches for his brown teapot. Thoughtful, he makes a pot of tea. Forgetting his naked-ness, he is drawn back to the window. Looking out but seeing only the past, he moves his body closer until he is almost touching the glass.

He thinks again of his bed-sitting room which over-looked a cobbled West London mews; remembers the posters pinned over the worst stains on the fading wallpa-pered walls. The Picasso. Two men with moon faces leaning against each other, weighted in space by heavy brown suits and solemn eyes. Van Gogh's yellow chair bright against a turquoise background. And over the door the poster he'd made with Rosalyn. Green and red and yellow handprints, Rosalyn's smaller than his.

Stepping back from the window, he reminds himself that all of this is nearly twenty years ago. Twenty years and still today. Pouring tea into a green mug, he remembers last night.

The telephone call had been brief. Rachel had broken the news.

Ralph had died two days ago. In a hospital side room, it turned out, before a hospice bed had become available. She was with him at the end. It was very peaceful, she has to say. He would have wanted me to phone. John had thanked her very carefully, and then hung up.

So that's it, he thinks. A life is over, done with.

Worst was the thought of the bleak hospital room with the pitifully few possessions displayed in a public locker. It could not be easy to die in a room like that, to die anywhere.

He turns away from the low bay window which draws the garden close into the house.

Ralph's shadow has returned since then, but at safe times; when a tall bearded figure distant in a crowd stirs a memory; or at the moment he reaches for his past lover, turning the pages of an old photograph album where the snapshots secured by glued corners are black and white.

SUNSHINE

In a garden in the heart of the city the sound of bird-song, filtering through the summer air, seems curiously unreal. He sits very still. The sunshine which drenches his whole body is benevolent. He wonders whether to go back upstairs and change into shorts... But his saturated being, lazy-blooded with the heat, doesn't want to move.

When he opens his eyes, he sees Steve kneeling in front of him, naked except for a faded pair of cut-off jeans. Teased by the deliberate tear which exposes the pale low curve of a buttock, John blames the summer afternoon for the desire that stirs so unexpectedly within him.

Afraid his feelings will escape and glide like fingers along the tender ridge of Steve's shoulder, he tries to think of something else, reaching through the haze of emotion for the sound of bird-song that had led him there. But all he can hear now is the snip-snip of the hand shears as Steve clips and tidies the ragged flower border. He stands up.

'You're not going?' Steve wipes the glistening sweat

from his forehead with the back of his hand.

I must, John thinks and smiles nervously.

'Relax. Take your shirt off.'

Now this is the last thing he can do.

'I could lend you a pair of shorts,' Steve says.

'I've some of my own.'

'Go get changed then.' Steve turns back, bends down on his knees again with the shears.

Of course he doesn't find me attractive, John tells himself. Hesitating, he knows instinctively that if he does go back upstairs to his own flat to change, his desire will humble him, make him feel too self-conscious to return. He will be reduced to sneaking glimpses of Steve from his living room window.

'Holidays soon,' Steve says, over one shoulder. 'Will you go away?'

'Maybe...' What about you, he wants to say, but resists.

Steve resumes his cutting of the grass.

'You seem happier,' he says. 'Hopefully the worst of the year is behind you. After the break-in. And everything.'

It's the first time Steve has even fleetingly referred to Jeff's leaving. John notices how even now Steve is shy of using Jeff's name.

The summer air stills. The last trace of any breeze dies away as though their small part of the earth has stopped breathing. Abruptly, the quiet in the garden is broken by a shrill burst of bird-song.

'Things are better,' he says with an effort. He does not mention Ralph's death. Nor the feeling that there is someone else out there. Someone he has yet to face.

'Glad to hear it.' Now Steve smiles. It is a nice smile.

They look at each other. Both wanting suddenly to speak. A telephone dimmed by distance — windows, doors and walls — rings. The moment vanishes.

'Your phone,' Steve says helplessly.

Naturally, the ringing stops as soon as John enters the flat. He blinks, his eyes adjusting to the dim, windowless hallway. Going into the kitchen, he runs the cold tap, fills a glass with water, gulps it down like a child.

Unzipping his jeans, pulling them off, he notices how pale his legs are under the dark hairs. He'd never been a sunshine fan, had always avoided, to Jeff's annoyance, the beach holidays. Reaching in a drawer in his bedroom for the grey shorts with the blue stripe, he catches sight of his reflection in the tall bedroom mirror.

His silhouette is no longer that of a boy, or even a young man. The years have thickened his waist, threatened a belly. The bush at his groin, the hair that weaves in finer trails from his umbilicus to his burnt pink nipples is touched with grey. There is an extra layer of flesh over his shoulders, down his back. Even his thighs and buttocks are heavier. Smaller framed, with finer hands and feet, he will never have Ralph's god-like proportions, but it is still a body solidly male.

He turns, considering the glass. You can never escape... he realizes. You can only tread water, trying to keep your chin above the waves and wait until the tide gradually takes you further away.

HOME

The sun filters through the leafy roof of their den, casting bright dots of sunlight over Suzi's frail back.

Leopards... he thinks, holding his breath and imagining big cats with black spotted fur stalking the jungle on padded paws, their claws sheathed. Only this picture draws him back to the awful reality of what is happening. For Suzi — eight years old, boney-chested, wearing only pink cotton shorts and scuffed sandals — is crouched with a knife in her hand.

How can she terrify him, this scrap of a sister he towers over? After all, he is strong enough to drag her arm behind her back and take the knife away. Perhaps what stops him is his own fascination, the curiosity creeping behind the horror.

Suzi pauses for a moment, her grubby hand clenched around the knife handle.

'Shall I?' she asks.

Now he could take over, he finds he cannot speak. His

mouth goes dry just like when Miss Pearce stops his heart, silencing him absolutely with a question about the algebraic equation chalked on the blackboard. And just like then he has the unexpected desire to urinate, release his water in a long satisfying stream.

Only yesterday Blackie, their pet goldfish, was swimming from side to side of their aquarium, oblivious to the rainbowed gravel and the plastic diver with the round brass helmet investigating the green weed. But this morning Mum had come downstairs and found Blackie floating belly upwards. Perched on wooden stools, shaping the sugar-coated Weetabix, neither of them had noticed that the fish tank was empty until Mum had said.

'I want to see him,' Suzi had demanded. 'I want to see him dead.'

If only they'd buried him. Everything dead should be buried with a proper gravestone or a Holy Cross so that whatever had died couldn't come back and haunt you.

'She's flushed Blackie down the toilet,' he had told Suzi first of all, perhaps because that was his own fear.

Maybe one day when he was standing to have a pee, or worse, when he was sitting there unsuspecting on the cold seat, not only Blackie but all the pets anyone in the street had ever owned would creep back up the pipes and float glassy-eyed in the scented blue water at the bottom of the pan.

Ever practical, Suzi had peered down the toilet disbelieving. Later that afternoon, she'd discovered Blackie wrapped in newspaper underneath the potato peelings in the round tin dustbin.

And so now, crouched on the dirt floor of the den, walled in by hedge and leaf, the two children sit with the dead thing between them. Suzi picks Blackie up in her left

50

hand. He doesn't know how she could even have touched it. Poised with the knife, Suzi contemplates what exactly will happen when she cuts off Blackie's head.

Although he has a front-door key in his pocket, he does not use it. Even though his mother is expecting him, it seems too much of an intrusion, simply stepping in after he'd been away for several months. He gives the doorbell a long ring so that he will be heard even if she is in the garden, pottering with a trowel.

Almost at once the door opens as far as the security chain allows. His mother stares at him round the side of the door. She is wearing her brown-rimmed reading glasses. As she lets him in, he sees she is still carrying a folded copy of the *Daily Mail*.

'The crossword,' she says, gesturing with the paper. 'I'm stuck on nine down. Agitated. With five letters.'

He kisses the cheek she tilts absently towards him then follows her down the familiar hallway with the coastal watercolours and the mahogany barometer no one has even tapped for years.

'You've grown your moustache back,' she says, over her shoulder. 'Whatever made you do that?'

He shrugs self-consciously.

'I fancied a change.'

Checking his face again, his mother smiles.

'Cup of tea, love? I've just had the kettle on.'

For supper they have cottage pie; mince and onion topped with mashed potatoes and grated cheese. Other than a cube of Oxo she uses no herbs or spices.

'I put extra butter with the mash,' she says, when they sit down at the table in the dining room. 'Blow the cholesterol.'

She gives him by far the biggest helping, serves the carrots and peas from a separate dish with a steady hand. Besides his plate is a can of lager and a glass. She will only ever allow herself a small sherry before dinner to take her mind, she says, off the cooking. She has always expressed the fear that alcohol reduces human beings.

Sitting down, his mother unfolds the red paper napkin she has put out especially for the occasion. She waits for her son to shake the small bottle of brown Worcester sauce over his pie, just as he had thirty years ago when this was his favourite boyhood meal.

'If you don't mind afterwards,' she says, 'we can watch the vet on television. It's a repeat of course, but I forget the stories.'

He nods.

'Your father was Lancashire born,' she reminds him later. 'Kirby Lonsdale. He lost most of the accent when he moved down here.'

Like much that is said within a family, he has heard this before. He half smiles at her as she collects the dinner plates together. Tomorrow they will be closer, he thinks. Merely staying overnight in this house will help, as though waking in his old bedroom he will be her child again.

In the morning bright sunshine streams through the window on the stairs down into the hallway where he catches his mother standing in front of the hall mirror. Wearing a simple white and pale blue cotton dress with a low waist, she is experimenting with a wide-brimmed straw hat. Perhaps it's just the change of clothes, but today she seems fifteen years younger.

Hearing his footsteps on the stairs, she turns and smiles up at him.

'You don't have to come,' she says, lightly. 'I was going to let you lie in.'

'I'd like to go with you.'

Again, his mother smiles.

'You know,' she says, 'this hat is nearly forty years old and back in fashion. Should I risk it?'

He offers to drive the metallic grey Ford Fiesta, but his mother prefers to take the wheel, protective of this last piece of independence. 'It's not often I have the chance to drive anyone anywhere,' she tells him, her white summer shoes deft on the pedals.

He breathes in her perfume. The sun is fierce through the windscreen as they turn round a bend. His mother peers through her owlish sunglasses and he blinks, sits back into the seat and closes his eyes.

Slowly, as though coming out of a dream, he can feel the green fern feathered under his fingers and the prickle of the stiff grass. There is a twitch along the length of his bare arm that might be a beetle; but he doesn't look. He can hear Suzi's voice, but far off, calling out to Dad. For a blissful moment he is alone in the wood.

As the sun reaches into him, he stretches out flat on the grassy bank, wanting to feel he is part of the earth, his arteries and veins running underground, making him a giant. Closer too, he hears the sound of running water, the gurgle where the stream ran over the dark rocks that he'd hoped would be his path across. But that way is too uncertain — the water too deep — and so he waits. Lying on the grass, a fringe of fern tickles his brow. Enjoying his solitude for the moment, he knows that even now they are looking for him.

If he stayed here for days, he wonders, would he turn from a boy into a tawny-skinned woodman, lean-muscled with a dark beard? The thought excites him. He wriggles against the earth, happy, suffused with the sun.

'There you are.'

He looks up. Mother seems to float down beside him, graceful in that never-seen-before white and black polka dot dress. She is wearing curved sunglasses like butterflies and, unusually, red lipstick. A cloud of perfume surrounds him as his mother moves to sit down, teasing the hem of the simple summer dress, carefully avoiding creases as she finds her place on the long grass beside him. Lightly, her hand reaches out and strokes his forehead in a gentle, caressing way his body remembers for days afterwards.

'What a lovely day,' she says, half to herself, and the sigh in her voice catches him, seeming to come from a private world of her own he had never suspected before.

The car swerves sharply round a sudden bend in the road. He rocks forward in his seat, blinded by the dazzle of the sun fierce through the windscreen.

'Nearly there,' his mother says, dropping down a gear as the car steadies its pace up the slope of the steep hill which leads to the edge of town.

They separate, as though by arrangement, at the tall wrought iron gate.

'I won't be long,' his mother says.

He nods reassurance and watches her retreat, a cool figure in white and blue, taking gentle steps along the narrow grassy path that snakes its ways through the horde of cement crosses and marbled tablets which mark the resting place of the dead.

Taking a different path, he walks slowly round the edge of the graveyard, close to the hedge and the tall flint wall. Besides the grave of Gwendoline Redding, a covering of green crystal chips enclosed by a white marble frame, he comes across one of the few creaking wooden benches. He sits there for a while, enjoying the heat of the sun, closing his eyes, lulled by the bird-song.

Later, he finds his mother sitting on the edge of his father's grave, legs crossed but relaxed as though she were perched on the corner of a bed, chatting to an ailing friend.

As soon as she is aware of him behind her, she gets up and smiles away from him. He sees that she is happy, can feel the play of her feelings about her like water. He remembers Suzi saying how she'd once caught mother laughing here as though she and Frank had again shared a joke.

'I'll leave you for a moment.' She begins taking steps away, not saying goodbye or making any sign. If she does talk to her husband it's never so he can hear.

The irises she'd picked from the garden stand blue and yellow-hearted in the grey stone pot, their quill petals like sharp feathers. Reaching out, he touches the headstone with his father's name.

Everything in the garden shed is just as Frank had left it; the leaning rake and long-handled broom, the tattered wool sacks filled with rags, the black Wellington boots in the green trug under the improvised workbench with its surprisingly miniature metal vice. Along one wall sag the homemade hardboard shelves supporting bags of fertilizer, seed containers, bottles, the empty glass fish tank. There are upturned hardward chairs, the bulky black bag with fishing tackle, a ringed net and Frank's last bicycle with five gears.

Behind the striped deck chairs he has come looking for, hanging from a nail is Frank's handyman suit. John looks up.

A far-off summer's day. His father kneels on the doorstep of the house painting the front door bottle green, perspiring slightly in his blotched blue overalls. Tongue-tied, he shuffles his feet and his father, aware of the audience, turns and smiles at him.

'Take the brush, son,' his father offers.

He shakes his head, afraid perhaps of failing in some way. Just eight years old, he wonders what it is like to be a man. Would like to touch the reassuring solidness of his father, smell his shaving soap.

Never one for conversation, Frank turns back and continues with his work, a perfectionist making even brush strokes.

High in the crystal blue sky the afternoon sun seems to set the grass on green fire, burning everything to silence. His mother sits back in the striped deck chair, perhaps asleep, the round dark glasses shielding her eyes, her arms resting down the arms of the simple chair, palms open as though awaiting benediction.

Beside her, John looks down at the flowerbeds, the orange and red marigolds, the blue irises and sapphire lobelia, the tall white tufted flags, the red and purple bells of fuchia, the tender apricot of the roses that climb another wall. He thinks of the garden he might have if he leaves his London flat for a home in a Northern town. He likes the idea of a house, of somehow starting again.

Comfortable in his shorts, bare-chested, he feels the warmth of the sun radiate deeper into him, making him sigh. There is a feeling suddenly that he'd forgotten, a sense of hope fluttering like a butterfly caught between a child's cupped hands.

It seems just then that he has escaped. That the only past which pursues him is a gentle and forgiving one. But he cannot stay here forever. He must still go back.

His mother coughs and he looks at her. She smiles at him, her dark glasses making her seem blind.

She is sure that Jeff has left him. For the last few months only her son has answered the telephone in London. He never speaks now of Jeff, deflects any enquiries.

Her son's vulnerability both moves and frightens her. It is a relief to be finished with certain kinds of love. She shivers as she thinks this because she too can still be bruised by dreams that steal in from nowhere in the small hours of the night. Frank...she thinks.

She looks down at the garden which has become her consolation. Perhaps tonight, she wonders, at the dinner table John will tell her what has happened. She wishes she knew how to initiate this conversation without hurting him; whether it was better not to say anything at all. It is partly nonsense, she thinks, this perception of age bestowing wisdom. And whatever happens, there is still a meal to be prepared.

His mother reaches out and touches his forehead. As she stands up, John sees how much of an effort it is for her now to get up out of a low chair.

'I'll cut a rose,' she says. 'Just one for the table.'

He watches her go, threading her way a little stiffly across the shimmering lawn. Holding his breath, his mind clicks like a camera shutter, trying to seal her in time forever, protect her from that last surrender.

Whatever their ending, past lovers usually meet again. Most often awkwardly.

JEFF

Jeff, inevitably, arrives late.

The dimly-lit gay pub he'd suggested as a rendezvous is deserted in the early evening. Nevertheless, the two men don't kiss when they meet and are nervous of sitting too close to one another. John recognizes from last summer the white trousers Jeff is wearing, but the navy canvas shoes and the canary yellow shirt are new. To his dismay, Jeff has had streaks bleached into his fair hair. He is uncertain what any of these changes mean.

'I wasn't sure you'd turn up,' Jeff says defensively.

John wonders how he could think that. After the weeks had run into months waiting for a letter or a telephone call. He realizes nothing is understood between them.

'I'm glad you rang,' he begins, then founders.

Jeff takes a tentative look at him.

'You've caught the sun. It suits you.'

'I've been sitting out in Steve's garden.'

Jeff raises an eyebrow.

'The motor fanatic downstairs?'

John nods. He wishes he hadn't said Steve's name.

'Drink then?' he offers.

Jeff glances around the bar, appraising in one moment the few men there. It re-occurs to John, like something forgotten because of its very familiarity, how attractive Jeff is; how easily he would draw attention and desire. This thought makes him feel even further away, like some shabby man whose advances could not possibly be wanted.

'I tried to give you space,' he says.

'I know.'

Jeff pulls at the shoulder of his yellow polo shirt. Suddenly he seems to have lost his edge of confidence. He wonders if he should have suggested they meet for a meal in some hushed restaurant. The food, the fuss with dinner things, the decor even, would have been a distraction. There would have been less chance of an unpleasant scene and, at the same time, the dinner-table atmosphere would have provided an immediate sense of intimacy. Now he simply has to try and create this with words. He realizes he is still a little afraid of John. He's surprised by the lack of power he feels on making this comeback. Turning the jade signet ring round on his finger, he tries to unravel what exactly he is feeling at this moment. After all, that is why he is here.

'Were you bored with me?' John asks, hearing curiously the echo of his sister, Suzi, in his tone.

'We were used to each other.'

Jeff hesitates. John sits forward in his chair.

'The usual, then?'

Jeff nods.

As John rises to go to the bar, for the first time they catch each other's gaze. The look between them burns for a moment.

61

Perhaps there had been passion between them. At least at the start...

He frowns. Time, as much as memory, conceals particular details, blurs motives.

PARIS

It could have been the twenty-first century. The absence of anything familiar, only the pale, pitted, cavernous walls. Perhaps they are at the heart of a volcanic eruption, a vomited vault of stone, and running through it just the silver grey snake of an escalator track.

Curiously empty of people the mechanical pathway threads its way through the softly lit stone labyrinth. At any moment you might expect twenty-first century people to appear, looking much the same as their antecedents, but dressed in those mysterious, seamless clothes that don't have buttons or zip-fasteners, as though in the future what we wear will at last have become a second skin, infinitely preferable to the frail reality beneath the fabric.

The escalator winds its smooth way forward. The textured walls, which were at first so odd, become restful, perhaps because of the very absence of posters and bill-boards, the tease of advertisements. Eventually other figures appear on the escalator, men and women standing yards apart, isolated with their suitcases.

Silent, they come at last to a glass building, dissected diagonally with numerous mechanical stairways, like a vast hotel where the residents, suspended or lost, simply stand and look out from the ceaseless intersection of moving stairs. An intermediate world perhaps, a place of transition. It is, in fact, the Charles de Gaulle Airport. And they are in Paris.

They stand in the stone-tiled square outside the Cathedral of Notre Dame. Wandering closer under the shadow of the two towers, they play with the sharp sense of perspective the building imposes. Jeff walks at last to the farthest side of the square, still threaded with tourists even on this chilly autumnal day, and takes another photograph.

'Everything in,' he says, grinning. 'Bordered by square and sky.'

A tall, slim figure with a shock of blond hair, the high collar of his trendy, black, loose-fitting coat is turned up against the cold. He seems so young then, less even than his twenty-five years, like a student almost. Watching him, nearly a decade older, John becomes preoccupied, aware suddenly of his extra years. Turning, he studies the cathedral quietly.

Three of everything, he thinks, wondering at the Holy Trinity; the Father, Son and Holy Ghost, none of which he quite believes in.

There are three arched doorways at the front of Notre Dame and above these three windows. Two of these are arched, but the middle window is eye-catchingly circular and intersected by thin lines of stone like a spider web. In front of this round window are three stone figures as close to each other as singers in a harmony. Between the windows and the doors is a long line of solitary stone figures, each standing in their own narrow alcove. Man after man, of course, all in long robes, stern arms folded across chest after chest. Saints, perhaps.

John wanders closer to the tall doors. They will sell guides inside... A group of Swedish teenagers emerges suddenly, blond after blond talking excitedly to each other, kept in a bunched, jostling order by their mature shepherd-teacher. Jeff grimaces as these youngsters collect at the entrance doorway with their garish shoulder-bags and instant cameras and exuberant self-confidence. He cannot then abide the company of anyone significantly younger than himself.

'Shall we walk on?' he says. 'We can go inside another quieter time.'

John nods, content with this. It has stopped raining now and in the late afternoon, a watery but still welcome sun throws its last light down on them. As they step across the grey square, he is aware of the flapping of wings as a scurry of pigeons swoop down on the crumbs scattered by a laughing little boy.

They are naked together. The strange bed in the unfamiliar room seems to demand some sort of christening. Perhaps it is the call from those countless other lovers who have lain or cried there. Now as visitors to the capital, seeking their own aphrodisiac, some sort of effort is required. John makes love carefully in the darkness, but a little later loses his way.

'You can fuck me...' Jeff says, unexpectedly.

So far in their short affair, he has been shy of this act and John, uncertain of his new role of older man, has been reluctant to press his young lover.

The hesitation, the fiddle and awkwardness, the compromise between urgency and tenderness, helps put him off and he loses his hardness as he'd feared. He tries to disguise a yawn, wanting suddenly to sleep, but Jeff is determined. Perhaps he believes that this act at last granted, planned even, is necessary to draw them closer. Cunningly, he uses his mouth until John is hard enough to try again.

Afterwards, John holds Jeff very close, kissing him gently, brushing the fragile bones in his shoulders with his lips. Grazing the side of the upturned face with his fingertips, the young, lithe body shifts slightly within his arms.

'*Was it good?*'

The hushed question, anxious in the darkness, pulls and tugs at him. Was his voice asking Ralph... was other voices, more than he ever wanted, and now this...

He wonders where all their fear comes from. Whether the emptiness inside everyone ever goes away whatever the kisses and caresses. Knowing it is all he can do, the best attempt at completeness, he holds Jeff closer, not drowning this time, but treading water.

They wander along the busy Boulevard St Michel where the bruised elegance of the buildings reminds John curiously of Edinburgh. Even in the centre of the city the arching houses, turned over now to commercial purposes, still retain something of the grace conjured by the architect of an earlier time. Regretfully, now the cafes of other decades are interspersed with jeans and clothes shops exactly like those in any other European city. And McDonalds has crept in.

The Parisian crowds, wrapped up in autumn coats and scarves, do not look quite so strained or push quite so hard as those in London. Crossing the road loud with traffic, they come to the high wrought-iron gates which herald the relative peace of the Luxembourg Gardens.

Jeff is happier today. He even woke with a smile, John thinks. As they cross the road, Jeff runs a hand down John's back. Bumping shoulder to shoulder as they step along the wide path, Jeff scans John's face for a smile. John remembers how he'd once been like that, so eager for closeness.

Somehow whatever had happened last night in their hotel room — the awkward, even animal coupling — did matter. At least today Jeff glows with it. Knowing this only increases John's sadness.

'Smile,' Jeff says.

He does his best, hearing the click of the automatic camera as the picture is taken. No one has taken his photograph for many months. It is one thing he hasn't missed.

They walk on together, down the terraced steps to a wide, enclosed ring of water with a sculptured fountain. Impressive in the sudden sunlight, the Luxembourg Palace stands before them, quietly grand like some stately home.

It occurs to John that he is grateful for Jeff's company, that perhaps he does not need this young man's love. For a moment he takes Jeff's hand.

They meander through the gardens, wandering along the grassy paths which lead past the tennis courts where the enthusiastic players step and scurry in colourful tracksuits, agile against the cold. Jeff wishes they could go back to their hotel room so that John could make love to him like last night. It had felt so good then, that bewildering mix of sensations which went beyond the merely physical; the discomfort which becomes a pleasure.

He was mine then, Jeff thinks. Even as he moved inside me, I possessed all of him.

Underneath his long coat and black jeans and briefs, he

becomes hard again. He wants to take John's hand and lift his coat and put it there.

They visit the Musee d'Orsay, a gallery of nineteenth century art which has been set up in a refurbished railway station overlooking the Seine River.

Wandering down the cool white stone steps to the first hall, open like a foyer, they admire the sculptured figures of lovers and gods. From there you can look up and see suspended the vast, gilded station clock. Through the roof of arched glass a grey light falls, conveying a sense of calm. Threading their way up and down pale stairs, they pass along pastel corridors admiring the works of Degas, Renoir, Pissarro and Monet.

At last John finds the painting he has been looking for. It is a large canvas with relatively few colours; yellow, black and cream. Three men kneel in an empty room, poor workers in a once-grand house. Each man is stripped to the waist and wearing dark smudged trousers. Through a glass doorway light is cast down onto their bare backs. The leanness of the men, their hunger, is emphasized by their long arms reaching forward with tools which they are using to scrape old paint off a wooden beamed floor. Two of the men are speaking to each other as they work side by side. The third, perhaps the oldest, kneels on his own, intent on his work.

He first saw this painting on a smaller scale. A reproduction of the Caillebotte hanging on an upstairs wall of a stone house. A stone house which overlooks a canal.

He shudders.

As he manoeuvres the naked young man onto his back, Jeff looks up into his eyes.

'What about me?'

Immediately, John doesn't understand.

'Maybe I would like to fuck you?' Jeff says.

These words alone push John away from the bed. Standing up, he pulls the now ridiculous condom off his abruptly flaccid cock. Stranded in the confines of the hotel room, he realizes he doesn't want to allow Jeff this intimacy. That even while he holds the young man, plays the protective role of older lover, he is determined to let Jeff get only so close.

Disturbingly, he can remember too clearly other seemingly insignificant moments with other lovers. His resisting an exploring hand, rolling away at a certain physical moment, making it clear silently that sexually his was the active role.

Had he made it like that because he was afraid, because the hurt that was his legacy from another — not seen yet — was never truly forgotten. Determined not to be so vulnerable again, he would not let anyone enter him.

Rising from the bed, Jeff steps up behind him.

'It doesn't matter if you don't do that,' Jeff whispers. 'I'm happy with you inside me.'

He reaches down for John's cock as though providing proof of this wish, and in that moment seals his particular sexual fate.

It is too late for regrets, but his breath still catches in his throat.

Because all of the time with Jeff there was that other ghost standing unspoken between them. That other figure behind the hesitancy and the silences he had never properly explained away.

JEFF

Stepping to the bar, he smiles automatically at the barman.

'Bacardi and coke,' he says, hearing a hundred echoes.

'Ice and lemon?'

He nods, lost for a moment, staring at nothing. He looks up, aware of the short, moustached barman hovering.

'And a pint of bitter,' he adds, completely forgetting his intention to stay sober on mineral water.

After he returns to the table with their drinks, they sit and talk in wandering sentences about work, the weather, mutual friends; nothing which at that moment touches them. Aware that the minutes are slipping through his hands, John wishes he could hold back time. He thinks of the long-dead comedian Harold Lloyd, pale-faced in black-rimmed spectacles and a dark suit, hanging suspended from a height, struggling with the arms of a giant clock, kicking wildly in the air, finding no foothold.

'How is Suzi?'

'Well enough. Busy with the kids.'

Jeff nods.

'I expect she told you you're better off without me.'
John makes his face blank.

'She never liked me,' Jeff says.

John hesitates because this is true.

'We're buying a flat,' Jeff announces.

'We?'

'Paul and I.'

So there was someone else. It is the first time Jeff — or indeed anyone — has mentioned this name.

Why did you leave me? John suddenly wants to ask. Did you feel I was too old? Did I bore you? Does Paul have a bigger prick...? He takes a swallow of beer. He isn't sure if his hurt is due merely to the loss of someone he once possessed. Certainly, he'd trusted that Jeff would always love him. Whatever his own feelings, he'd held onto that.

'Are you buying together?' John tries to calm his voice. Which Paul? he is thinking. A Paul he knows?

'That's right,' Jeff says, stiffly. 'A joint mortgage.'

He looks away. This had always been a point of contention between them. That the flat belonged to John. That he was simply the lodger who could be evicted at any time on a whim or after an argument.

John frowns.

'It was always really your home,' Jeff says, again.

'We lived together. I was committed.'

'*Were you...?*'

How suddenly they are vulnerable. Their words shake them. They turn away from each other.

I was afraid... John thinks. But he cannot say this. The fear is still there inside him.

At any moment time could turn in on itself, take you back to places you never left entirely behind. Once again he stands in that tall, stone house. Lost on the giant staircase, with darkness everywhere.

How foolish he'd been to think he could hide. Part of him must have known all along just who was waiting for him in the shadows. It was not Ralph who had haunted him, but the lover who had come later. The one he had waited years for.

Again, he sees Colin's hands moving up and down the black and white piano keyboard. The rapid motion of his stabbing fingers. He takes a breath. The tall house by the canal reaches for him.

COLIN

It was a year when wide-flared trousers were 'in' and the tips of broad collars reached the far edge of shoulders. Awful to remember now. Somehow the confidence of the Sixties had evaporated. Fashion was only half-heartedly followed, yet if the Seventies was the Grey Decade, the popular music of this time still had a leftover prettiness. Most likely that evening the Stylistics or Abba were harmonizing from the jukebox in the corner of the gay pub in Islington.

What makes Colin stand out is his thick green tie. Everyone else is sweltering in tee-shirts. Some of the men gathered there have undone buttons to the waist and stand with their chests stuck out.

Colin has a mousey handlebar moustache and dark eyes that reveal nervousness. His crisp white shirt still bears the creases from the iron. Self-consciously, his hand pulls at the wide knot of his tie which he does not have the courage to take off in front of everyone.

Their sex is less than spectacular. Colin is nearly forty, but timid. John, twenty-eight now, takes charge of their intimacy, perhaps even entering Colin that first night.

'First time I've ever fucked an intellectual,' he jokes, intending simultaneously to distance Colin and make him smile.

Instead a frightened look comes into the dark eyes. Perhaps that's what does it. For some reason John's caught.

'Don't ring me,' he says, in the morning. 'Just be here tonight. At seven.'

Colin nods. He too feels something is happening.

'You will be here?' John says again. Their urgency quickens their hearts. The moment when they say goodbye hurts.

As Colin sits upstairs on the double-decker bus which takes him back to his friends in Muswell Hill, he celebrates Fate which has come to save him.

John cannot remember when he has been so happy. It's as though this other self which has been struggling for so long inside him is at last free. As his emotions make a giant of him, everything else shrinks and becomes of small significance.

They spend most of the weekend in bed. They pretend dress and undress again. John wonders that this new body is his. Shorter and heavier, still Colin knits to his own shape exactly.

Taking it in turns to make endless pots of tea, they bring the hastily rinsed cups back to bed on a tray. Colin is a Lecturer in English Literature in Norfolk. They talk for hours about books, debating the merits of Forster and Lawrence, reading each other lines from T.S. Eliot and Auden, arguing whether Thom Gunn is over-rated or

William Golding unfathomable. Colin admires *The French Lieutenant's Woman* by John Fowles. John has discovered Margaret Atwood through her novel, *Surfacing*... and the talk goes on.

'It can't end...' John says.

Colin reaches up, his muscular arms weaved with dark hairs. He smiles, wanting John inside him again. He is unsure of everything, blocks out everything except these feelings. It is a sort of delicious oblivion.

'You will love my sister,' John says. They are walking across Hackney Downs on a warm September afternoon. The light streams through the leaves decked with leaves so green.

'What does Suzi do?'

'She wanted to be a model. Did some catalogue shots which went to her head, posing with a snake for the sleeve of some LP. Now she's at art college doing something, she says, for her soul.'

Reaching out, they graze fingertips for a permissible unnoticed moment.

'Does Suzi know you're gay?'

'Oh yes. She says it bores her. Partly, I think, because she's slightly bewildered by my lovers. A docile girlfriend would have been easier prey.'

'She sounds formidable.'

'She is.'

They walk on, the lowering sun reaching down through the line of trees, dipping them in gold.

'This comes just once,' John says.

His overwhelming certainty seems to make Colin sure.

It's as though John has provided him with a springboard and for the first time in his life, in nearly forty years, he can jump.

Built with various shades of grey stone, the tall house is mottled like a sea shore and has a sloping black slate roof. Its wide bay windows overlook a canal which runs quietly, a glimmering ribbon, along the opposite side of the road. Beyond the water there is simply countryside.

By the front gate, John puts down his weekend holdall, turns round and just looks. Through a wall of hedge in the far field a black and white cow appears. He starts to laugh.

Inside the house there is a vast lounge, a drawing room complete with a grand piano, and a long dining room. Every room in the house has high moulded ceilings and original fireplaces that are five feet high and patterned with beautiful floral tiles. Spare of furniture, each of the arching rooms gives John a sense of walking onto a theatre set. Even the staircase at the end of the hall is immense with heavy carved wooden bannisters and giant steps going up and up and up.

'I can't believe you live here on your own,' John teases. 'Where are the three bears?'

Colin shrugs.

'There used to be two lodgers. Students from the university.'

'You could practically fit the whole of my flat in your living room.'

Colin hovers uncertainly.

'Don't you like it?' he worries.

He wishes he could tell John that he'd felt safer back in London, in John's flat. There are too many memories here. Too much that is still unsaid. He looks very carefully around the long living room. Nothing seems to have been disturbed. There is no sign of violence.

Sloping away from the house the garden runs on for maybe a hundred metres before ending apparently in a line of trees. But this in fact is only the top garden. The next, flatter and with a leaf-roof like a glade, is dominated by a vast weeping willow that casts down drooping curtains of fine leaves. On one side there is a garden shed — the size of a small bungalow — and a tall hedgerow which hides what once was the vegetable garden. Here brambles and spider webs have now taken over everything.

From this furthest point the house is completely invisible. John breathes in the sense of peace. There is the sound of birds, a calling song and a flapping of wings, and the hum of a drowsy wasp. No human voices disturb the quiet. Absent too is the muffled chatter of a neighbour's television or the rumble of traffic from the road. After the business and bustle of London the silence of the countryside is almost deafening.

Colin leads him back to the green enclave of the weeping willow, a child's hiding place.

'Will you be happy here?' he asks.

Without answering, John takes Colin's hand. His London life — his home, his friends, his teaching post — already feel lost to him. Tears prick the backs of his eyes. Love has done this. And there is no way back.

He draws Colin closer. They kiss tentatively, moustache grazing moustache, their hands still clasped. Perhaps for a moment they believe, the world stands still.

After a discreet telephone call Colin's old friends and neighbours, Jan and Frank, invite themselves round for a drink.

Jan, a round Norfolk woman in her early fifties, sits on the sofa with her large gin and tonic, managing to fill even the vast lounge with her energetic chatter. Today at an autumn fete she has been taken up into the skies by a helicopter and naturally is still full of the occasion. Frank, her thin, older husband — the Laurel to her Hardy — sits silently beside her, perhaps thinking of Colin's garden and the lawns which he cuts for a small fee.

It is a sociable evening. After a few blunt questions she says she couldn't help, Jan is warm and welcoming. Colin, at moments, even takes John's hand. For the first time to an audience the two men discuss their plans to set up home together.

John makes an effort to include Frank in the conversation. They laugh a little at each other good humouredly. Jan makes a great show of extolling the virtues of Fenland life as opposed to the corruption and crampness of a London existence. 'There's room to breathe up here,' she says, waving her arms. 'And good clean air.'

It grows late. At a lull in the chatter, Colin disappears into the kitchen to prepare some percolated coffee.

Through her round owlish glasses, Jan's eyes turn thoughtfully to John. There is one question she hasn't asked. Her smile for the first time vanishes. She leans forward, her voice hushed like a conspirator.

'You do know about Tony...?' she says.

VOICES

'It will feel like home.' Colin tries to sound reassuring.

John nods and begins taking his bags up the giant staircase of the tall stone house, dumping them in the corner of the second spare bedroom which is destined to be his study.

Less than seven hours ago they had been in London. At the last his flat was completely empty, just like the deserted shell it had been before he'd brought life into it: painting the walls, fixing the curtains, putting up pictures and shelves for books. As they'd had a farewell look round the flat their voices had echoed unnaturally loud. There was nothing left to deaden such sounds or soften them.

Now, more than anything else, John feels like a refugee, someone whose life has been left behind. Surrounded by all these huge, half-empty rooms, the sense of vulnerability is almost overwhelming. He is unable to forget the fact that this strange, cold house belongs to someone else. He wonders who had chosen the carpets or the pattern of the paper on the walls. Perhaps he is standing in a home that Tony had made.

Watching him from the doorway, Colin tries to remember how sure John had been when they'd first met. It occurs to him how much he had relied on that certainty, ventured even to depend on it, and yet the young man in front of him now stands as quiet and sad as a stranger.

Colin shivers because there are things he should have said before now; because everything he had hoped to escape from still lies waiting for him on his return.

He hesitates as John walks across the empty room to the tall window and looks out. He realizes he doesn't know what to say.

They make love quietly in the dark. It seems to help a little. Eventually they drift off to sleep. Perhaps all they need is time.

But less than an hour later they are disturbed by a loud ringing which reverberates through the whole house. Someone is leaning on the front doorbell. Someone determined to be heard.

In the dimness John can just make out the shadowy figure of Colin stepping to the window, pulling back the curtain just a fraction, peering out. Without even asking, he knows. It is Tony out there.

A narrow set of enclosed stairs leads the way to the two large attic rooms. Moving the beam of his torch, Colin at last locates the light switch.

Blinking as the light flickers on, John sees in one room a spare mattress piled with folded blankets and coverlets. The other room has a makeshift dressing table with a stained mirror and a chest of drawers. But taking up most of this second room are twelve or fifteen stacked boxes and half a dozen bulging plastic bags. Colin frowns at this collection which is already covered with dust.

'These are the rest of Tony's things.'

John shakes his head.

'Why didn't he take all this when he went?'

Colin looks away.

'There was no room for anything more in his new flat,' he says quietly.

John tries to keep his voice even.

'So how long has this stuff been stored here?'

'Eight, nearly nine months. Since he moved out.'

There is a silence. Both men are nervous of what they might say.

'Is this everything of his?' John asks in the end. 'Absolutely everything?'

Colin avoids his eyes.

'There are some plants that belong to him downstairs in the drawing room. I couldn't just let them die.'

John takes a deep breath, wondering what else he doesn't know.

'We have to talk,' he says.

There is a telescopic spy-hole in the front door whereby in a good light you can check the identity of any caller standing on the doorstep. By arrangement when Colin's friends visit, they ring the doorbell three times; one long and two short rings like a code.

To make sure there are no mistakes, Colin shows John a photograph. Tony looks harmless enough really; thirtyish, wide-faced with quite nice eyes and a close-trimmed red beard. The fact is this man, who is even smiling in the

82

snapshot, has blacked Colin's eyes, bruised his ribs and twice threatened him with a knife. And all this when they were lovers.

In the days that follow John is drawn into a peculiarly adult game of Hide and Seek.

Whenever they go into town, shopping or visiting the cinema, Colin keeps looking over his shoulder. Whether it is in the busy pedestrian precinct or the car park, John acts as look-out. Once as Colin pulled out of a parking space in a side road, Tony had thrown himself across the bonnet of the car, battered on the windscreen.

The room which is intended to be John's study is shabby and in need of attention. Determined to keep busy, John decides to make renovation his first task. When the room is transformed he will have at least made some mark on the house.

He starts off replastering around the window frame and above the skirting boards. Then he replaces the worst of the tattered wallpaper and covers everything over with four coats of a warm, yellowy buttermilk emulsion. Afterwards, he sandpapers the skirting boards, the picture rail and the door, and then carefully glosses them brilliant white.

All the time he works, each of the hours and hours, part of him is tensed, waiting for the hammering at the front door.

Colin is sitting at his office at the university when the grey telephone on his desk rings.

'Me again,' says the caller.

Colin pretends bluffness.

'What do you want now?'

'Just a chat.'

'I'm meant to be working.'

'You'd rather I called round at two in the morning...?'

'You promised you'd stop that.'

'Well then.' Tony pauses. He knows he must stay calm, keep his voice level. He has a deep, warm Humberside voice other men have often admired. 'You never made Friday lunch,' he says lightly. 'I was waiting in The Cricketers half an hour.'

'It was difficult getting away,' Colin half lies.

'Never mind.' Tony allows himself to be understanding. Sometimes that's the best way. 'This Friday then,' he says softly.

Colin wriggles in the hard chair.

'We can only talk...'

'O.K.' Tony half wants to laugh, but then stops himself. 'I only want a chat,' he says. 'Just to see you. No harm in that, is there, not for friends?'

'No...'

'Friday then. Same time.'

Tony hangs up just as Colin is about to speak.

One afternoon the first of Tony's handwritten notes comes. Pushed through the letterbox. Waiting for them in the hall.

The anger creeps into their voices.

'We were lovers for four years,' Colin says. 'I can't just suddenly cut him dead.'

John forces the words out.

'You're supposed to be committed to me.'

Colin steps further away, closer to the tall window. He

looks out, his breath misting over the cold glass, endeavour-
ing to steady his voice.

'When he moves to Carlisle to live with Michael, all this
will stop,' he says.

He gazes down at the garden, at the bed of dried-up
bronze hydrangea and the gnarled apple trees. He tries to
remember what it had been like those first days in London.
What it was exactly he believed he'd found with John. It all
seems so far away.

Turning round, he faces John just for a moment.

'You must trust me...' he says.

In the darkness they hold each other as if they are afraid,
making love without really looking into each other's eyes.
They kiss numbly as though their bodies are too bruised for
passion. Every caress is sad rather than sensual. They touch
because it is all they have left. But they do not speak.

Just as they have begun a meal, made a special effort with
wine and candles, the telephone in the hall rings.

Colin gets up from the table, goes out into the hall, picks
up the receiver, listens for a moment.

'I'll take it upstairs in my study,' he calls out.

As his footsteps retreat up the stairs, John tiptoes out
into the hallway, picks up the telephone receiver resting on
the hallway table. He hears the click as Colin lifts up the
telephone extension on his desk.

'How did you get this number?' Colin begins.

'A little bird.' Tony's voice is surprisingly gentle.

John shudders.

'Ringing me at work is one thing, but not here...'

Tony interrupts.

'This is urgent, Col. I had to speak to you. Carlisle's fallen through.'

Colin takes a breath.

'If you and Michael have had another row, you'll make it up. You always do.'

'Not this time. He doesn't want me to move in with him anymore.'

Tony's voice trails off.

'Anyway,' he begins quietly, 'perhaps it wasn't meant to be. Michael always said I was never really over you.'

There is a longer pause.

'But it was you who left me...' Colin manages.

Again, Tony breaks in.

'I didn't know it would turn out like this,' he says. 'That you'd run off to London and find someone else.'

Another silence. Colin chooses not to answer.

Downstairs, cold in the hallway, John holds his breath.

'It was fun last week.' Tony's voice is different again, softer. 'Perhaps we can see more of each other,' he says. 'Now I'm not going to Carlisle...'

GHOSTS

The music starts suddenly. They are standing in their chosen corners of the hall, slightly self-conscious, waiting for some sort of cue.

The instrumental sound streaming through the huge loud-speakers is slow and dream-like. Most of the group in their brightly coloured leotards and sweatshirts realize that this is the Sleeping part. Some of them slump forward, their hands trailing the ground, as though while bending down to touch their toes they have for some inexplicable reason dozed off. For the two women with long unbound hair, this posture is particularly effective. Several of the others in the group slowly get down onto the bare polished floorboards and curl up in a foetal position. Watching them carefully, John lies prone as though he is in bed, his head cradled on one arm.

'Imagine you are on another planet, another world, another time...' instructs the tall woman by the powerful cassette-deck.

The fifteen people in the room do their best, some frowning with concentration, even though they are still on the planet Earth, and gathered, more precisely, in the upstairs hall of the Zorba Dance Studio.

As one might expect the women in this Creative Dance Class outnumber the men two to one. There are two lithe pretty boys in their teens who from their fleeting improvisation obviously also do ballet, jazz and tap classes. Then there is a ginger-haired bespectacled man in his thirties whose long white limbs extrude from his cut-off jean shorts and tie-dyed shirt. The oldest participant is a round-bellied man approaching fifty who looks like a banker who's taken an afternoon off work and squeezed himself into a grey monogrammed sweatshirt and tight green shorts.

The women, ranging from eighteen to forty-seven, are more fashionably and colourfully dressed in pinks, yellows, greens, purples, reds and blues. With the exception of the two pretty boys, the women are by far the most flowing and unself-conscious of the dancers. But the other men try hard. As the music reaches the germinating theme, everyone begins to get into their stride.

Arms and, with more difficulty, legs become roots and tendrils, twisting their way up through the dark forest earth towards the light. Photosynthesis, muses John, drifting back to 'O' level Biology classes, sprouting bean-shoots and a chunky teacher called Graham Pratt he realizes now he had a crush on.

'Rising from the earth, at last you can leave the sanctuary of the womb,' the dance instructress shouts encouragingly. 'Each of you is becoming more and more alive.'

Now the electronic wavering gives in to drums and percussion and a more urgent, native beat. Everyone in the room does their best to go Savage. Again the women as a whole are much better at this. The two teenage boys, however, go into a stunning routine, whirling and circling round to meet each other, then shying arms flailing, away from each other's grimacing faces. John watches them enviously, wishing he'd been as sure as that at seventeen.

The music changes again. Something sinister and creeping is happening. Nearly everyone at once goes into spiky, spider movements.

'You are hungry,' wails the instructress. This is obviously her favourite bit. 'You are alone and you need to eat. You search for your prey. You capture and devour them. Only then you are *twice* the size and *twice* as hungry...' Her voice rises to a stagestruck shout. 'You won't be satisfied until you have eaten *everyone*.'

The effect this has on the group is electric. At first no one wants to be devoured, preferring instead to menace. Then the pot-bellied banker, who quite fancies the woman in the silver-blue tights, decides to be captured (hopefully by her). As he makes his wriggling death-throes, the rest of the dancers see the extravagant possibilities there are to being eaten.

For a while everyone is eager to fall in front of the path of the ever-increasing monster, which soon becomes a balletic rugby scrum of rainbowed arms and legs. The throbbing music rises to a crescendo. There are just three of the group left, running in circles, crossing and crisscrossing in front of the juggled-together creature, taunting it. John thinks suddenly of Tony's voice on the telephone. *All the lies...*

One of those still free, he finds himself running in front of the monster, stamping on the boards.

'You are angry,' shrills the instructress, picking up on something. 'Your fury is building up into a storm.'

The monster rages on. Everyone is sweating profusely and getting tired now, but they are determined, despite their aches, to end the evening in style. Closing in on John, their last adversary, they get ready for the kill. Dashing in close to their feet, he hammers on the boards with his hands, shouting even, lost for a moment in his own private world.

As he is caught he kicks out, struggling too roughly for play, before the monster, protesting at his violence, loses a multitude of footholds and falls on top of him.

He is alone in the tall house. Colin has gone away to London for an academic appointment and is staying over-night with his friends in Muswell Hill. He had not asked John to accompany him. There is the feeling, unspoken between them, that he is relieved to get away.

Wandering out of doors into the top garden, John sits down on the sagging wooden bench and looks around at the shrubs now brown-leaved and shrinking with autumn. He tries to remember how he'd felt seeing the garden for the first time. He can recall Colin wandering down with him across the bright lawns, reaching for his hand. It had seemed then that they had everything to look forward to and nothing to fear, as though their love had made them safe.

Now he is suspicious every time the telephone rings. Every morning he endeavours to be the first to reach the post, scooping the letters up, searching for that spidery hand. Tony continues to write spasmodically. At the break-fast table, Colin reads these letters quietly and then takes them away and says he destroys them. John doesn't know what to believe.

Pursued by doubt, he meanders slowly down the gar-den, raising one hand to grip the lowest branch of the apple tree, pausing to look up at the twisted black limbs. He did love me... he thinks. Turning, he stares back at the grey stone house which towers above him. Lately, he has drifted like a ghost from one aching room to another, diminished in some way by the love he believed in and which now seems so insecure.

Was I just an illusion... he wonders. Someone who quite by chance at a particular moment seemed so much more suitable than an uneducated lorry driver who had no interest in literature or classical music, and was awkward when there were colleagues from the university gathered round the dinner table.

As the afternoon light begins to fade, John stands very still. There is a November chill in the air. The richness of the deepening blue autumn sky fills him with a shivering sense of ending. He saw now that Colin had never truly been free enough to love him, only there was no law which said you had to be free to love.

Stepping through the gap between the hedge, he stands in the middle garden dominated by the giant weeping willow. Moving round in a wide ring, his hands trail through the skirts of leaf. He wonders if it is all too late, whether there is any hope left.

Suddenly something makes him turn. Has he glimpsed movement out of the corner of his eye? Once or twice before Tony has come through the back way into the garden. His mouth dry, John forces himself to look slowly around him, at the long shed, at the shrubs tall enough to obscure an intruder. In such a vast garden there are so many places to hide. Walking quickly up the grassy slope back to the house, he half expects a figure to suddenly appear, to find Tony standing there, loitering beneath the apple trees.

Safely inside, he sits down at the top of the stairs, shakey with relief. Not so long ago, he'd sat there listening to Colin playing a Chopin sonata on the grand piano in the drawing room. He makes himself remember the first time he'd heard Colin play when it had seemed as though Colin was making the music just for him. He wonders where exactly Colin is at this moment. What is he doing? Who is he with.

He hopes Colin will ring this evening. After all, it is his first night alone in this house.

Standing up, he looks out of the mid-stair window onto the fields. The autumn sky burns now, the red searing the purple against the cloud edge of gold that is the dying sun. Soon it will be getting dark.

Nervous of catching sight of a figure standing in the shadows, he draws all the curtains early on. And then at once imagines Tony standing listening on the other side of the chill glass.

Later on, the telephone rings and he runs to it. But it is Tony's voice.

'Is Colin not there then?' Tony sounds as if he doesn't believe him.

'He's in London,' John says defensively, and immediately regrets it.

'At Nick and Dave's, I suppose.'

John hesitates, wondering how Tony knew this, hating his own vulnerability. Words stick to the roof of his mouth.

'So John...' Tony says softly, 'I was hoping we would get round to having a chat.'

He lies in bed waiting. It seems inevitable that tonight of all nights Tony will come.

Turning over restlessly in the wide bed, he glances at the illuminated figures of the alarm clock. Nearly midnight. He wraps the duvet closer round him as if it is a magic cloak that could protect him.

Faint comes the sound of footsteps from the road. The rustle of someone possibly pushed against the hedge. He strains his ears. Later, just as he drifts off to sleep, there is the creak of the wooden gate. Caught in the wind, perhaps.

As strange light flares through a chink in the curtains. There is a crackling sound like the snapping of twigs and a rushing noise which could be a high wind. He sits up in the half darkness, knowing suddenly.

The house is on fire.

He wills himself to move. He must try and get out of the room, but his eyes are blind now. He takes a breath and his throat burns. Stumbling out of bed, he reaches out through the smoke, working his hands along the wall of wardrobes to where the door must be. Frantically, his fingers seek the brass handle. Finding it, he swings the heavy door open, only to see the flames.

They are everywhere. Fiery tongues of red and orange licking up the walls, bright against the black smoke. The sheer heat forces him to step back...

Raising his hands to his face, he begins to scream.

PACKING

At nine years old Sean is mostly past the hand-holding stage. Irritated if he is mistaken for the boy's father, John is quite relieved by this. He suspects that there will soon be a time when his nephew will no longer want to come swimming with him, only this thought makes him sad. He will miss their outings to the local pool.

As usual John lets Sean decide whether he wants to undress in the individual cubicles or the communal room. When he was five and John had started teaching him to swim, Sean had paraded quite unself-consciously in the communal area. Now, perhaps due to the influence of the school he goes to, Sean often prefers the cubicles.

Today the boy leads his uncle into the communal area. Halfway through changing, Sean whispers to him, 'Everyone will see us.'

John slips off his checked shirt, touches his dark moustache.

'We're all more or less the same,' he says. 'Give or take

a few inches or a little fat.'

Sean looks about inquisitively at the men of all ages in various stages of undress.

'Some are hairier too,' the boy says. 'Will I have hair like that?'

'Not until you're older. It also depends on what you inherit from your father.'

Sean considers this carefully.

'Daddy's not as hairy as you,' he says.

He looks up at his uncle. He would like to reach up and stroke the thick chest hair, run his small fingers through it. But even at his age he is aware that this is not permissible.

Once in the pool, Sean naturally enough enjoys showing off.

'Watch me dive,' he cries, racing to the deep end.

As always, John is relieved when the boy surfaces again, choking and spluttering. It's impossible to shake this feeling of being responsible for a child. He dives in himself, then breast strokes carefully to the shallow end, knowing from habit that Sean will follow in his wake. After two proficient lengths, Sean is bored with the adults.

'Can I go over to the slides?'

John treads water.

'For the last ten minutes. First shall we practice the front crawl?'

This is both their weakest strokes and Sean is quickly impatient with it. He is itching to shoot like a rocket down the slide which ejects the fun-loving into the deepest end of the warmer children's pool.

'Mr Wessex says I should do the crawl like this,' Sean protests, keeping his face down in the water, coming up spluttering again.

'Then I should do it the way Mr Wessex says.'

'What about you?'

'I'm too old to change.'

'I like it your way.'

'As you wish.' John makes the pretend hippopotamus wallow which Sean still loves, and wonders at the way children debate everything endlessly.

'Do it again... *please.*'

John obliges and then Sean experiments floating on his back, before his head turns once more in the direction of the excited children's voices.

'Is it the last ten minutes yet?'

'I think so.'

Sean streaks off with barely a backward glance.

'Coming?' he calls from the pool side.

'I'll watch,' John shouts back.

Sean nods seriously. This is their usual arrangement.

After the swim they sit in the cafeteria by the long window overlooking the blue water. John has a black coffee and Sean a fizzy limeade and a packet of cheesey Munster Claws which he arranges neatly on the formica table top, checking each of them for their authenticity. In between crunching the savouries he talks mainly about school and the computer he's using now. The degree of technology coming into the Junior school classroom still astounds John, even though he is now having to teach his own pupils similar skills. Remembering his own childhood when calculators hadn't been thought of and there were literally coloured blocks to help counting, he feels even closer to middle age.

Sean pauses to consider his uncle, remembers something he'd been wondering about.

'Has Jeff gone on holiday?'

The question startles John. He is never quite sure what Suzi has told her son, how much he understands. Still, the boy knew that Jeff lived with him. Perhaps he should have said something before.

'Jeff has moved away,' he says.

'Where?'

'Another part of London.'

Sean considers the largest of the cheese claws which he has been saving until the very end.

'Will I see him again?'

'Maybe.' John deliberately checks his wristwatch, taking his nephew's attention.

Sean grimaces.

'Do we have to go?'

In case he's missed anything, John makes one last inventory of the flat, checking the drawers and cupboards a second time. Going through the bookcase again, he takes another four books off the shelves and adds them to the pile of possessions he's already packed into several cardboard boxes in the centre of the room.

Everything in these boxes either belongs to Jeff or was bought by Jeff for both of them. There is not so very much there. John wonders if that was his doing. Most of the domestic things — the pots and pans, the settee and armchairs, even the pictures on the wall — he'd already owned before he met Jeff. Perhaps he'd never really let Jeff make too much of an impression on the flat. Even when he had redecorated, whilst he'd consulted Jeff about the choice of paint and paper and drapes, he had always paid the bills himself, ensuring (he supposes) that it always remained *his home*.

He sighs.

What a mess it all seems. Just as Ralph had come into his life too early, at a time when commitment had been too confining, so Jeff maybe had arrived too late.

Through Colin he had lost something. Not his innocence exactly, but that impetuous, almost naive belief in love. He shakes his head. He sees at last that with Jeff he had always tried to play safe, had never risked giving himself completely. Whatever had stopped him was part of Colin's legacy...

He still dreams of the tall stone house. Wakes it seems to find himself in Colin's study, running a hand along the tops of the orange-spined paperbacks, catching himself standing at the top of the giant staircase waiting for the piano notes. At other times he wanders in the gardens like a ghost, leaving no footsteps on the grass, his spectral hand disturbing the skirts of leaves.

PROMISES

He'd left the postcard, an Impressionist landscape, face up on the wide desk in the book-lined study.

Will you come and live with me... Colin had written on the back.

He steps across the landing to the opposite room where only weeks ago he'd laboured, painting the walls buttermilk and white. He runs his hand along the marble fireplace he'd spent hours working on, stripping off layer after layer of brown paint until at last he'd come to the polished stone.

From the tall window, he looks down at the highest part of the garden, at the gnarled branches of the apple trees and the banks of grass where only a week ago he'd knelt and planted the tulip and daffodil bulbs whose blooms he will never see.

Yesterday they'd walked along the canal, past the old stone bridge. Here, as the narrow path gave way to nettles and water-logged mud, Colin had stopped him.

'I just don't know what I feel any more,' Colin says. He shrugs as though this frees him.

John keeps his face calm, even while his whole world collapses inside him. Perhaps no words will ever hurt as much as these.

'And Tony?' he asks.

'You were right.' Colin looks down at the canal which reflects the black reaching branches of the leaning trees. 'Something there just isn't finished yet,' he says.

'So you don't love me...?'

Colin never answers.

Gathering together the little that is still his in bags and boxes, he packs again what he'd unpacked less than three months ago. He has both found happiness and been, it feels, betrayed. He has lost two homes in just ninety days. He will never completely trust love again.

Last of all before he leaves he looks again at the postcard on Colin's desk. An Impressionist landscape with an inscription on the back. Words of love and promises that mean nothing now.

He pauses on the stairs, the emptiness of the stone house all around him. He looks down at the tall front door. Even now he wants Colin to return, but there is no jolt of the key in the lock, no chance for any reunion. So he will go quietly, without even any argument.

He hesitates in the hallway, hearing the muted ticking of the clock, nothing else. He takes a breath.

He would like to burn the whole house down.

He remembers how later he'd cried just once, in front of everyone on the train back to London, but not again, not until months, and even years afterwards, when the tears come back at the most unexpected moments. For no reason it seems.

THEFT

He looks into the mirror, low on the bedroom wall, and this time what does he see.

The antique shop perhaps, the dusty one he and Jeff had stumbled upon down a narrow side road in Camden Town. It had had an old-fashioned coiled brass bell which rang as you entered and rows of china dolls and moth-eaten teddy bears, Japanese vases and Coronation china set out on long wooden shelves. The shop had been completely empty of people, though there was so much clutter you hardly had room to move. Every step you did venture threatened to overturn a precarious display, a sleeve catching on a Dresden arm or an elbow nudging the petalled rim of a glass light shade.

From behind a rolled Persian rug an elderly man summoned by the bell appears, dressed in a mustard cardigan and a white shirt with a thin brown tie. Nearly seventy, red-faced (possibly from drink) he peers at them over half-lenses, one hand smoothing back his grey, greased hair in the face of custom.

The tall mirror with the gilt vine-leaved frame stands at the back of the shop behind an oil painting of gold chrysanthemums. Jeff sees its possibilities at once, how the present furniture in John's bedroom could be rearranged so that the mirror was shown off to its best effect.

Now, as he stands quite alone in the bedroom that is just his, the afternoon light begins to fade. Other shadows creep in.

The dimly-lit bar is draped with gold and silver tinsel. Suspended from the beamed ceiling, over the clusters of chairs and tables are paper Santa Claus and snowmen. The piped music is a never-ending medley of Christmas records; everything from Bing Crosby to Cliff Richard and Wham. Sitting on a bench seat, John toys self-consciously with the lunchtime menu card, trying to relax. Every year Christmas becomes more unreal to him.

Opposte him, Jeff slips off his black leather jacket and hangs it on the back of the hard chair. He smiles at John as though at an old friend, someone completely safe. John sees he has kept the highlights in his blond hair. He still does not like them.

'Where did you get the tan?' he asks.

Jeff smiles again, confident how well he is looking.

'Tunisia. We had a short break a month ago.'

Unable to help himself, John conjures Jeff and his new lover in some strange hotel room, the light coming through the wooden slats of the shuttered window, striping their lean, brown bodies.

'Still in the classroom?' Jeff rearranges the roll-neck collar of the white sweater which makes his tan seem darker than ever.

'Frantic home-made Christmas cards, end-of-term reports and carol services,' John says. He frowns in an effort to appear detached. 'How is the shop?'

'Quiet. But then we usually are at this time of year. Pictures are the sort of present people prefer to buy themselves. Business will pick up with the January sale.'

Jeff thinks that this is something he must have told John a dozen times before. Perhaps that is the danger of any relationship — there is only so much to say.

'How's Paul?'

Jeff hesitates.

Immediately, John regrets his words. The question had risen from nowhere.

'Fine,' Jeff says.

In fact they have quarrelled lately.

Do you love him, John wonders. He suspects Paul is younger and more handsome than he is now. Than he will ever be again.

'What about your love-life?' Jeff leans forward as he says this, sipping his Bacardi and coke.'

'Non-existent.'

John smiles to soften this, touches his dark moustache.

In fact the time he spends in bars has become a habit he both wants to break and relies upon. Always careful with his drinking, he sticks to a regimented limit which will leave him relatively sober. Sometimes he enjoys merely observing the comings and goings of the other gay men who drink there. At other times the whole procession bores him. He has seen it all before; the affairs and the trysts which come and go, the posing and the posturing.

Occasionally, he sees a man who attracts him, but he does not act on such feelings. Perhaps there are too many defences now, too many paths he has already trodden. The older you get the easier it is to anticipate endings, and the harder it is to hope.

He says nothing of this to Jeff.

Draining his tall glass, Jeff, suddenly awkward, avoids John's gaze.

'There's still some things of mine in the flat,' he says, quietly. 'Perhaps we can fix a date when I can come and collect them.'

John swallows.

'Why not collect them now?'

Jeff is taken aback.

'This afternoon?'

'Yes.'

Suddenly it is imperative that he gets Jeff back to the flat. He rises to his feet as if this has already been agreed. More slowly, Jeff slips his black leather jacket back on. He is not sure where this will lead and uncertainty always makes him feel uncomfortable.

He wonders if he returns to the flat, whether John will try to make love to him. This possibility, contrarily, is reassuring. He wishes he had taken up John's offer of another drink.

Jeff hesitates in the hallway like a visitor to a strange house. Yet he can simply glance into the kitchen and still remember one drunken afternoon years ago now when they'd made love there, slipping and sliding on the brown and cream linoleum floor, their naked bodies greased with practically a whole bottle of cooking oil. The glistening hardness of cock against cock.

He realizes he has drunk the two Bacardis on an empty stomach. Now his desires runs dangerously.

Numbly, he follows John into the living room, watches his ex-lover pour the whiskey into two chunky glass tumblers. Taking the glass passed to him, Jeff sits down on an armchair, crossing his legs to hide his erection.

Now Jeff is back here, John tries to think what it is that he needs to do... He takes a sharp swallow of whiskey. Do I really still want him? he wonders, as he sits down on the wide settee. Or is it just the past attempting to displace the present...?

Looking round, Jeff realizes that John has changed the room. Not drastically. The wallpaper and the curtains are still the same, but little things are missing. The green china bowl of pot-pourri, dry rose petals and lavender. The Japanese cushions on the settee. Gone also is the framed photograph of the two of them on the bridge in Florence, the Hockney swimming pool print and the white Pierrot mask that was a birthday present. Even the bookcase looks emptier. Perhaps John has sold or set fire to the books he'd left behind.

It bothers Jeff how uncomfortable he feels. How he'd always felt that there was something which John kept from him. All at once he is able to turn his regret into resentment. He tells himself that John has begun to look his age. The black moustache has grey in it, his hair is thinning. He's heavier round the waist now, thicker-thighed, and there are tired lines cut into his face.

'Another drink...?'

John sits forward, but Jeff is already on his feet. Is he going to leave, John wonders.

'I'll get them.'

Jeff steps towards him. As he takes the heavy tumbler out of John's hands, their fingertips touch for a moment, then shy away.

Standing by the sideboard, pouring the whiskey into the glasses — just as he had in this same room a hundred times before — Jeff looks out of the window which is abruptly swimming with rain. It had rained that afternoon in Ambleside on their first holiday away together in the Lake District. The hills deserted, the green of the grass was like velvet, the purple of the bracken soft as one of those mauve jumpers knitted by an aunt.

Their inappropriate track shoes leaking water, they'd steamed inside their blue cagoules, their hair flattened against their heads in the downpour. Cold-handed and warm-tongued, they had kissed on the hillside, not minding the rain.

He thinks how once perhaps they had loved each other. But the memory is inconvenient. Whatever it was that John had withheld in the past was not wanted now. Jeff realizes he too has changed. There is no longer that innocent hope of Paris. Cynicism and evasion have crept it. Suddenly even thirty feels old.

He adds a spurt of tonic water from the nineteen-seventies siphon to the whiskey in the glasses, just as John kisses the back of his neck very lightly, inhaling the latest aftershave from Yves St Laurent.

Slipping his arms under Jeff's shoulders, John folds his hands across Jeff's chest, pulling him closer in a bear-like embrace. He isn't sure whether this is lust or loss or loneliness. Perhaps now everything is impossible, motives cease to matter. Perhaps all he wants for a moment is to hold on. To have the comfort of another man in his arms. But Jeff, stirred by the echo of their past sex, reaches behind him, his long fingers blindly trying to find and unbutton John's jeans-fly. John shudders at the touch, aware not only of what he feels, but what, despite this feeling, is missing.

Sinking to his knees, Jeff frees John's cock from the tangle of cotton. And in that moment a sheet of glass, a window seems to come between them. John looks down at

Jeff as though at a stranger. Is this all they have left, he thinks. The lazy desire and the regret; the left-overs of love.

Jeff watches John take the four large cardboard boxes out of the deep hall cupboard. He sees that each has been securely tied with string and labelled with a list of contents. This orderliness of John's surprises him. He'd always put John down as disorganized; Dozey Doris, Dreamy Dora.

All at once he wants to forget their sticky intimacy. No sooner had they separated and adjusted their clothes, it had been terribly clear that they would never touch like that again.

Running his eyes down the neat lines on the boxes, Jeff doesn't really take anything in, wanting in fact to saunter around the flat and claim something else, cause some sort of disorder.

He argues constantly with Paul. He would like to make a scene now. Frustrated by John's apparent calm, he makes in just a small moment a decision that he will never in his lifetime properly review again; that John is cold, that it was this coldness which drove him into Paul's arms all those months ago. Always afraid, the limitations of life, those invisible bars at every window, seem closer still. He had, he tells himself, wasted six years of his precious youth on a cold and now ageing man.

John telephones for a taxi.

They do not speak while they wait for it to arrive. Perhaps there is simply nothing left to say.

Jeff goes into the living room and looks out at the late afternoon darkness. Winter has already settled down over the black slate roofs. The squares of light from the windows of the houses opposite give him no comfort, engender no curiosity. He starts at the sound of the bell rung from below by the taxi man. Quickly, he reaches out and takes a paperback off the bookshelf, one that he has never read which does not belong to him. Hiding the book inside his leather jacket, he walks out into the hall where John is waiting.

Together, making two journeys, they carry the loaded boxes down the stairs and out through the communal hallway into the street where it is still raining, the droplets chill on their faces. Without a smile, the taxi driver opens the boot of the car for them.

At last it is all done.

Turning up the collar of his leather jacket, Jeff steps into the back of the car with just a blank, backward glance. The door slams shut. As the car pulls away, its red tail lights winking in the dark, John raises his hand as though to say goodbye.

ASHES

Slowly, John dresses for the funeral, selecting a neat white shirt with a button-down collar. Over this he puts on a charcoal grey suit, the closest he can get to black. He hesitates over his choice of tie; black cotton, black leather or something lighter. In the end he decides on pink. Guy would like that.

The service is only minimally religious. Guy hadn't set foot in a church since he'd been a ten-year-old choirboy, curly-headed and pale-cheeked, slight even then. There are no hymns today. Just three popular songs Guy had specially liked broadcast through the discreetly placed loudspeakers.

Those who are gathered there do not attempt to join in with the singing, but stand in silence, remembering perhaps Guy in full drag, miming to the same songs they're hearing now. There are less than twenty present and almost all of them are other homosexual men. Guy's parents had been invited, but had declined to come. His sister, Becky, is there though, dressed in one of the clinging scarlet dresses Guy himself had once worn when performing some bar-room cabaret. The few who recognize the dress admire her for it. She stands in the front pew next to Chris, wobbly in stilettoes that might be hers or Guy's, and is the first to cry.

Throughout the service, John watches Chris from his place on the third row, fixing his gaze on the big man's shoulders, silently willing him to hold on.

After the third song there is a short silence which eats into everyone. They all seem afraid to look at one another. Then, breaking the quiet, is the swell of Hollywood strings. A panel in the wall opposite opens and the wooden coffin, draped in red silk, slides smoothly forward along the hidden runway and disappears. The wooden panel closes again. From offstage the dull red curtains are drawn.

It is an awful moment.

The music changes once more. Everyone stands very still, anxious to show their respect. One or two of them fumble in their suit or denim pockets for handkerchiefs. Others fix their eyes on the stone floor. There are men here who are terribly afraid. Men who are also remembering someone else who is lost. One wipes a tear along the line of his dark moustache.

John watches the shoulders of Chris's dark suit. They are very still, his close-cropped head bowed.

The final song is Ella Fitzgerald singing 'My Funny Valentine'. As soon as he hears the opening words, John realizes that this last must be the song that Guy had especially chosen for Chris. The exquisite voice sends echoes high into the vaulting space. The hairs go up on the back of John's neck. Chris turns round suddenly and stares straight back at him. There are tears in both their eyes.

He screws the last of the three hooks into the living-room wall. Already this afternoon he has fixed onto the same wall the wooden shelf which will support the various potted plants that are at present clustered on the carpeted floor, throwing leaves and greeny tendrils up to his knees.

Going into the bedroom, John has to stand on a chair to lift the tall mirror with the vine-leaved gilt frame away from the bedroom wall. Cobwebs he'd never suspected trail greyly in the air as he swings the heavy mirror down onto the floor.

Later, placed over the wooden shelf in the living room — suspended on the three hooks — the mirror does capture something of the sky from the window opposite. Certainly, the reflected light makes the room seem brighter. John arranges the potted plants along the shelf, pleased with his efforts.

He has just climbed into a warm, foamy bath when the doorbell of the flat rings.

Stepping out dripping, he covers his nakedness with his dressing gown, pads barefoot along the hallway, opening the front door to find his neighbour on the doorstep. Steve has lately shaved off his would-be beard, but left a dark moustache which quite surprisingly suits him.

He smiles shyly.

'I was wondering how you got on with your D.I.Y. this afternoon?'

John tightens the knotted cord of his dressing gown.

'It's all done. I was going to return the drill later.'

'There's no rush.' Steve flushes slightly. 'I'm sorry I've disturbed you.'

Suddenly John remembers the emerald and mauve sweater Steve had quite unexpectedly given him on Christmas Eve. And how, to his horror, he'd had nothing to give in return. Even while he is thinking this, he is abruptly aware that Steve is looking at him, is peculiarly certain that at this precise moment what Steve is noticing are the hairs on his legs, dark and wet. To his surprise, the two of them have stepped, blindly he supposes, into a sexual moment.

'You can come in,' he says, after a pause. 'And inspect the handiwork.'

Steve shuffles in behind him. Uncertainly, they wander into the living room. Steve politely compliments John on the straightness of the line of the shelf along the wall. To be honest, it seems a funny thing to do to him, putting a mirror on a side wall, not even over a fireplace, and then covering most of it up with plants.

But he does not say this. Instead he makes a suggestion.

'Perhaps you could get a potted hyacinth, something to add a little colour.'

John nods, even though it had been his clear intention for the plants to be purely green and leafy. He turns round and catches Steve staring at him again. The young man ducks his chin.

'I'd better let you get back to your bath,' he says quietly.

As John says goodbye and closes the door after him, he can picture Steve bringing him a bright potted hyacinth next week. He cannot think of any way of stopping him.

In the quiet flat in St John's Wood, the two men sit opposite each other listening to the hiss of the gas fire. They do not say anything as the tea in their ornately flowered teacups slowly turns cold.

John glances around the walls at the pictures which remain a curious mix of tastes: a still life by Bonnard next to a vast monochrome of Marilyn Monroe; a coloured abstract by Paul Klee besides a billboard poster of a Shirley Bassey concert. He wonders how long Chris will keep Guy's pictures alongside his own. When the memory will become too intrusive.

He looks across at the empty armchair closest to the flickering gas fire where Guy had sat in those last days, supported by pillows and cushions. With the assistance of two key workers from the Helpline and a district nurse (who Guy nicknamed Helga), Chris had managed to nurse his lover at home until the very end.

John sighs comfortably. His Sundays have become lazier of late. Growing used to living on his own again, gone gradually has been that anxious need to fill time. He has begun now to loiter through the hours, turning the pages of a novel, wandering round a chilly park in a coat and scarf, dozing off in the armchair in the middle of a hired Hollywood video. Pottering generally, hibernating his way through the wintry weekends, he is content to know that spring will come.

Now, as he listens to the steady tick of the antique clock, he can feel his eyes begin to close. It would be easy to let this Sunday afternoon simply slip away, but there is something he has to do.

Chris, a weekday office executive now hunched in a black zipped jacket, turns to look at him.

'I suppose,' he says, 'it's time to go.'

They are driven to Hampstead Heath in a black London cab. Shivering a little after the warmth of the flat, they wander down the narrow pathway which leads away from the small artificial lake where in the summer children and adults play with yachts with cotton sails and miniature radio-controlled powerboats. The trees that soon surround them are tall and black-branched, barren of leaves, but still beautiful. In the late afternoon there is a blanket of silence over everything. You can almost smell the mustiness of the wood.

Meandering on, they pass another middle-aged man in a leather jacket hovering under the trees. As they step close by, he tries to catch their eye in the hope that they are after sex.

All at once John feels sad, not for this man pursuing his lonely vigil, but for those other men who belong irretrievably to yesterday.

He can remember the Sunday afternoons of a decade and more ago — years before the virus — when he might leave the pub with someone who'd caught his eye across the bar. Someone who agreed without even speaking that this liaison would last for only a few hours.

Perhaps these trysts were sordid, brutish even, and yet there was also something essential about the liberties they'd take with each other. Sometimes they wouldn't talk. Sometimes they'd simply cuddle each other. On other occasions their conversation was as open and free as their sex. Secrets could be shared. Truths, at any other time suppressed, could be told. It was the very shortness of the hours that made them safe.

John sighs.

Of course, all this was years ago now, but he can still remember those muddled occasions, surfacing later besides a stranger, perhaps hearing from the corner of an unfamiliar bedroom the radio playing the Sunday Evening Top Twenty. Pulling on your clothes quickly, you knew without asking the moment when it was time to go. Goodbyes were rarely necessary. Yet anonymous as these encounters were, there were times when what had been shared was not forgotten, when it haunted you precisely because you could not go back.

The two friends walk further into the wood. The sky above them changes, the blue sinking into the beginnings of a sunset.

Slowly, the stream of pink deepens to a dusky rose centred with the glowing orange globe of the sun. The blue above falls to a grey. As the sun is swallowed, the feathers of cloud stroking the horizon burn red against a lemon background, the blue glows greenly, and higher still, purple creeps in.

John holds his breath.

For a moment it seems the sky is ablaze.

He wishes he could capture it, hold onto this moment for ever.

With Jeff he had sought to deny the chaos of love. Had settled for something less. And yet chaos had still crept in, undoing even this compromise.

The trails of cloud dissolve like smoke. The gold flares finally. The purple bruises the rose. As the descending blue darkens, blackness steals in.

Perhaps it is time to stop being afraid.

The light fades further, leaving a chill behind which makes them shiver. Soon it will be dark enough, John thinks. But his mind is wandering still like something elfin between the shadows of the trees.

'Chris...'

Their faces are pale now in the dark. He hears rather than sees Chris take something out of the Harrods bag he has been carrying. John senses he is trembling.

'Can you do it...?' Chris says.

John reaches out and takes the metal container which is cold to the touch. He hesitates.

'Just here.' Chris's voice is now a whisper.

Unscrewing the lid off the casket, John steps forward. Slowly, threading his way along the path beneath the trees, he tips out the dust onto the earth floor. He walks on in the shadows for perhaps a hundred yards before he is sure that the casket is empty. Turning up to the sky, he is aware of the first glimpse of stars. He can just detect Orion and the Plough. Through the blackness, he retraces his steps back over the ashes that are all that is left of Guy, to the still figure of Chris waiting for him.

'We didn't meet here,' Chris says. 'He just wanted it.'

AGAIN

Amberley Avenue even has trees in it. Suzi comments on this, adding that you could find similar tree-lined roads in Hampstead or Wood Green or Muswell Hill. John decides to say nothing, scanning the grey stone houses with their wide bay windows and neat front gardens bordered by hedges and low walls.

'They're probably all Tories round here,' Suzi says, in a dangerous mood.

She is about to add that everyone who lives in Amberley Avenue must be retired — who else would have time to tend their front gardens so carefully? — when the door of a house opens and a little girl comes out followed by a mother in red dungarees and long dangling earrings. Seeing the little girl, Suzi wonders how Keith is managing with the children and whether he has had to telephone his mother yet for moral or practical support. She does not like to think of her husband managing too well without her.

Suzi sighs. Having endeavoured to pour as much cold

water and doubt over John's idea of moving to the North of England, she has by agreeing to spend the weekend in Manchester involved herself possibly in even assisting this transition. At the same time she is flattered that John has asked her and not an ex-lover to accompany him. And, of course, she is curious.

It turns out that they'd parked the car at the wrong end of the road. Eventually they find number sixty-three, a semi-detached stone house with a rickety wooden fence bordering an overgrown front garden whose untidiness is exaggerated by the cultivated neatness of the neighbouring lawns. The windows of the house are black and curtainless. John is pleased the house is empty; he and Suzi will be able to wander round and peer in corners without any interruptions. Reaching inside his padded jacket pocket for the keys he'd collected from the estate agents, he is aware of some small excitement. Suzi, walking beside him, is just as eager to look.

The wallpaper in the lounge is faded red poppies on a once-white background. The bare floorboards are sound with no apparent bowing or damp. The wide bay window makes the room light and airy and draws the grass of the front garden close in to the house. You could put pot-plants in the bay next to the rounded glass, or install a bench-seat with cushions for a cat.

Suzi calls him from the door.

'Did you know there was a sun terrace?' she asks, forgetting not to be enthusiastic.

John follows her into what could be a dining room or study. It is a square room with a completely different feel to the lounge, but just as light. Next to a tall window is a paned door which leads out onto a sun terrace. Beyond this is a surprisingly large but neglected garden which runs very slightly downhill and is bordered by low wooden fences. At the bottom of the garden stands a greenhouse. Halfway up the lawn, catching his eye at once, is a cherry tree, its gnarled branches waiting for the spring.

Suzi opens the terrace door, steps out straight onto the long grass, wanders down the garden, then stops, laughing suddenly.

'There's even a fish pond,' she calls. 'But no water.'

John watches her, smiling. Already he is thinking this could be home.

An hour later they are still in the house, leaning now against a dusty wall of an upstairs bedroom. There is a quietness between them. Occupied with their own thoughts, each allows the house to make its presence felt, waiting perhaps for the ghosts to come forth.

It occurs to Suzi that what she had regarded as some makeshift fantasy could actually come true. John might actually come and live here. Hundreds of miles away.

John thinks about the cherry tree which he can see clearly through the window; black branched and twisted, burnt almost. It reminds him slightly of that other garden where there were apple trees and a weeping willow. He waits, but the thought of Colin, coming inevitably, does not disturb him this time. Perhaps there is no love there any more. Just the memory of a hurt. And he can live with this. Afterall, he has lived with this for years.

'What about work?' Suzi asks, soberly.

'I've already one interview for a teaching post. And it doesn't have to be Manchester. It could be Bury or Oldham, any of the satellite towns.'

Suzi avoids his eyes. Slowly, John reaches out and takes

her hand.

'Will you move away?' she says, because she has to ask.

Leaning closer to his sister, he squeezes her fingers. His voice is equally quiet.

'Maybe...' he says.

Another Saturday morning comes. He is sitting in an armchair with a second cup of coffee and the *Independent Magazine* on his knees when the doorbell rings.

Steve had kept his moustache. Today he is wearing blue jeans and one of those grey sweatshirts with the useless hoods at the back which were fashionable a few years before.

'Hi.'

They look at each other. I shall invite him in for coffee, John thinks.

'Sibelius,' Steve says, surprising him, for it is indeed a recording of the composer's First Symphony which is playing in the background.

John nods.

'My brother plays that sort of stuff all the time.' Steve shuffles his feet. 'I want to show you something.'

Shyly, he turns, hesitating for a moment before he makes his way down the communal stairs to his ground floor flat. Pulling his latched front door shut, John follows him.

'I've just made a pot of tea,' Steve says, leading the way into his kitchen, where John sees a conspicuous attempt has been made to clear up. Even the formica work surfaces gleam.

'Herbal,' Steve declares, stirring the contents of the teapot. He is confident that John drinks this sort of tea all the time. He steps away from the table.

122

'Follow me,' he says.

Opening the backdoor, which sticks a little because of the damp, he steps out along the passage into the garden which is still white in the shaded corners from last night's frost. Both their breaths are smokey in the air. He touches John's elbow gently and points.

There, rising from the uncut grass, amid the stretching green stems and leaves, proud and bright yellow trumpeted, are the first daffodils of spring.

It is a good moment.

The two men smile at each other. It would never work, John thinks. Indeed if it ever came to sex, Steve would most probably shy away.

He looks again at the daffodils. They'd planted the bulbs together one Sunday afternoon last October. It had been his own idea, perhaps because of that other time and the blooms he never ever did see.

The two men exchange looks. At the very least they can be friends.

When John opens his eyes he finds he is sitting on a high, narrow bed.

Even in summer the room is dimmer than he remembers, the brown carpet covered with dust. There is that curiously addictive aroma of rolled tobacco.

Looking out of the open window in front of him stands a young man completely naked, smoking a crooked cigarette, flicking the ash into an empty milk bottle resting on the window sill. Thick black hair hangs in a long swathe down over his boney shoulders. Narrow-waisted, the figure is as thin-limbed as a boy. John can even see the line of ribs running down his side as he turns suddenly and stubs out the roll-up.

Crossing the bed-sitting room, the young man reaches for a tangerine tee-shirt hanging on the back of a hard chair.

While he dresses, John looks around once more. Sure enough, over the doorway hangs the poster he'd made with Rosalyn. Green and red and yellow handprints, Rosalyn's smaller than his, arranged like flowers (their fingers petals) and underneath written in bold letters, the word PEACE.

Pinned to the opposite wall is the eternal yellow chair bright against a turquoise background. Next to the Van Gogh is a Picasso. Two men with moon faces lean against each other, weighted in space by heavy brown suits and solemn eyes.

Then he notices the National Gallery calendar propped over the mantlepiece. Remembers not only the year, but what day and month it is.

The young man ties the laces of his canvas shoes, goes out without even locking the door of his room. His footsteps echo on the stairs. John half wants to warn him what lies ahead, but that would be breaking the rules and, anyway, it is all too late.

He feels at once both the simple happiness of the young man and his longing. He watches him step lightly down the street towards Portobello Road and the thriving Saturday market stalls. He knows that somewhere quite by chance in the crowd, Ralph is standing. In just a short while, pursuing purely random steps, the two men will meet.

He half wants to be there. To see his bearded god again. But in the same moment he knows that he has lingered too long in too many yesterdays. It is time to let go.

He glimpses the flare of the tangerine tee-shirt as the young man is swallowed by the melee of pedlars, shoppers, beggars and tourists. He hesitates in a doorway, taking a breath, turning for just a moment, to look back.

His life, of course, carries on. His continuing good health remains a blessing. Wary of the Test, he touches wood.

Part of him still hopes for a lover and one more chance, but other things occupy him. That is the way of life.

Pausing in the hallway of his house, he looks into the tall mirror which throws back at him only the uncertain reflection of a solitary man. He smiles as he steps away, and the picture in the glass changes again.

Also by Timothy Ireland

WHO LIES INSIDE

Life seems quite ordinary for young Martin. He's 18, tall and deciding on whether or not to go to college. He's one of the best players on the school rugby team, but recently he's had to take on his most formidable opponent — himself. Inside there is something different about Martin and he doesn't want to admit it. He knows that he is in love with Richard, his classmate, but he has no one to confide in. Admitting his feelings could jeopardize the relationships that are most familiar to him. Yet repressing his thoughts means neglecting his true identity. Alone Martin must find his own way.

Winner of the 1984 Other Award.

ISBN 0 907040 30 6
UK £5.95   US $10.95   AUS $17.95

THE NOVICE

Donovan Crowther is 23 years old and still a virgin. Romantic and uncertain, he is drawn to London in his search for love. And from the moment he arrives in the capital, it's clear that whatever happens, his life will never be the same again.

"There is a hard-edged reality to Ireland's writing style which is often effective and prevents the book being a piece of romantic pulp"
— *Campaign*

"I found *The Novice* wonderfully sincere and felt and fresh...It's a lovely piece of writing" — Edmund White

IDBN 0 85449 089 2
UK £5.95   US $10.95   AUS $17.95

GMP books can be ordered from any bookshop in the UK, and from specialised bookshops overseas. If you prefer to order by mail, please send full retail price plus £1.50 for postage and packing to:

GMP Publishers Ltd (GB),
P O Box 247, London N17 9QR.

For payment by Access/Eurocard/Mastercard/American Express/Visa, please give number and signature.
A comprehensive mail-order catalogue is also available.

In North America order from Alyson Publications Inc.,
40 Plympton St, Boston, MA 02118, USA.
(American Express not accepted)

In Australia order from Bulldog Books,
P O Box 155, Broadway, NSW 2007, Australia.

Name and Address in block letters please:

Name _____

Address _____

_____

_____

_____